ROBIN HOOD

BANDITS, DIRT BIKES & TRASH

Robert Muchamore's ROBIN HOOD series:

ROBERT MUCHAMORE'S
ROBIN HOOD

BANDITS, DIRT BIKES & TRASH

HOT
KEY
BOOKS

First published in Great Britain in 2023 by
HOT KEY BOOKS
4th Floor, Victoria House, Bloomsbury Square
London WC1B 4DA
Owned by Bonnier Books
Sveavägen 56, Stockholm, Sweden
www.hotkeybooks.com

A CIP catalogue record for this book is available from the British Library.

ISBN: 978-1-4714-1282-0
Also available as an ebook and in audio

1

Typeset by DataConnection Ltd
Printed and bound in Great Britain by Clays Ltd, Elcograf S.p.A.

Hot Key Books is an imprint of Bonnier Books UK
www.bonnierbooks.co.uk

ROBIN HOOD

THE STORY SO FAR . . .

Once upon a time, **Robin Hood** lived with his dad, **Ardagh**, and half-brother, **Little John**. He was a regular kid, spending his days battling boredom in school and his free time practising archery or hanging with his bestie, **Alan Adale**.

Everything changed when Robin's dad got sent to prison for a crime he didn't commit.

Robin's half-brother discovered that his mum was the super wealthy **Marjorie**, **Sheriff of Nottingham**, and went to live with her, while Robin shot local gangster **Guy Gisborne** in the nuts, forcing Robin to hide out in Sherwood Forest and join a gang of righteous rebels led by **Emma** and **Will Scarlock**.

With his new rebel pals, Robin blew up cash machines, hacked computers, caused a massive flood, flipped a police car, rescued an old lady from a fire, crashed several motorbikes and became a social media sensation, with footage of his daring robberies getting millions of views.

1. ZANDER THE ZIT

Josie Longshanks and Robin Hood stood just inside the chunky wire fence that separated Sherwood Castle from its disused hunting grounds. Thunder drummed to the south and it was cold enough to see the two thirteen-year-olds' curling breath as they hacked at grass and weeds with machetes, then dumped the cuttings in a wheelie bin.

'How much more?' Josie asked, eyeing ominous clouds as she scooped up an armful of fresh-cut grass.

'Until the bin is full,' Robin said. 'You'd be amazed how much Sheila's chickens eat.'

'Those birds get treated better than us,' Josie complained.

'Until we marinade them in peri-peri sauce and eat them . . .' Robin pointed out.

Josie laughed. 'True, dat.'

Her expression changed to shock as her boot caught a hole hidden by the long grass. Her jeans and the back of her heavy coat got soaked as her bum hit the damp ground.

Josie peeled wet denim away from her skin as Robin gave her a hand up. 'And now my arse is freezing!'

Josie and Robin wound up staring at each other, their noses only centimetres apart. Their plumes of breath merged as Robin admired Josie's dark eyes and the tiny, near-translucent hairs on her cheeks.

They'd been together for a couple of months. It wasn't super serious, but Robin still found having a girlfriend weird. It felt like he was wobbling along the tightrope to adulthood, half excited and half wanting to go back to being a kid.

Robin thought he might get a *thanks for helping me up* kiss, but Josie took him by surprise, whipping her hand up and trying to squish the zit on his chin.

'Bog off!' Robin yelped as he stumbled back, almost catching the hole that had taken Josie down.

'You've got the biggest zit I've ever seen,' Josie teased, playfully grabbing the hood of Robin's winter coat to stop his escape. 'As your girlfriend, I have the right to explode it.'

'Weirdo!' Robin said, as he wriggled free and bounced against the wire fence. 'Why would you want to burst someone else's zit?'

'You're practically growing a second head,' Josie said, then hooked her foot around Robin's ankle, trying to trip him. 'Since you won't let me pop it, I'm going to name it Zander.'

'Zander the Zit,' Robin said, staggering away, smirking and remembering that his favourite thing about Josie was that she was unpredictable and always made him laugh.

As their laughter died off, they heard more thunder and a growing buzz from a quad bike approaching the castle on a track that ran parallel with the opposite side of the fence.

The main road through the forest between Route 24 and the rebels' Sherwood Castle stronghold was barricaded and heavily patrolled by police and Forest Rangers. This meant a safe journey to the castle from the nearby town of Locksley involved a lengthy detour on narrow forest tracks before entering castle grounds from the rear and crossing an abandoned hunting zone.

'That's Marion's Aunt Lucy,' Robin said, as a quad with a huge pink box on the back skimmed by beyond the fence. 'She's made the cake for the naming ceremony.'

Robin liked Lucy, and considered jogging to the gate a few hundred metres away to say hi, but the storm was closing in and Sheila would moan if they didn't return to the chicken sheds with plenty of green stuff.

'I think naming ceremonies are—' Josie began, as Robin resumed slashing at long grass.

Her opinion went unaired as a massive crash sounded nearby. Metal tore, branches cracked, then there were shouts. Three or four voices.

'That's not good,' Robin blurted, dropping his machete and turning to look through the fence.

The trees in the hunting grounds were too dense to see far along the winding track, but a haze of dirt wafted between the bare branches.

'Has to be Lucy's quad,' Josie said, as Robin tossed her a yellow walkie-talkie.

'Use channel F and call security at the back gate,' Robin told her urgently, snatching up his bow.

The fence had been built to keep beasts like tigers and zebras inside hunting grounds where rich idiots once paid to hunt them for 'sport'. Its four metres of heavy gauge mesh were topped with Y-shaped posts that held strands of brutally sharp razor wire.

'You'll get slashed up!' Josie gasped as Robin fearlessly scaled the fence.

But he had a gift for climbing. Josie became less fearful as her boyfriend snaked his muscular shoulders between the strands of razor wire, then tore his trouser leg, before balancing on the taut topmost wire and making a two-footed leap into the nearest tree.

'Josie Longshanks here,' she told the walkie-talkie. 'We just heard a massive crash inside the hunting grounds. Quad bike driven by Lucy Maid. Robin has jumped the fence to investigate. But there was loads of shouting, so I think it's a bandit trap. Over.'

A disbelieving rebel security officer came back through the walkie-talkie. 'Can't be bandits this close to the castle, Josie. But give us your exact location and we'll check it out.'

Robin made noise hurtling down between branches and out of the tree, but moved stealthily once he was on the ground. Just like the security officer Josie spoke to, Robin hadn't heard of bandits operating this deep inside Sherwood Castle grounds. But as he closed on the crash scene there was no mistaking a young man barking orders and an anguished shout of 'Hands off me!' from Lucy Maid.

Robin kept low as he squelched across the deeply rutted track. There were boot prints and drag marks where the bandits had pulled Lucy into the trees, and Robin made a quick study of her wrecked quad bike.

Its front wheels and steering column had been ripped away from the chassis. The rest of the vehicle had flipped and smashed into a tree stump. As plastic bodywork and rotten wood splintered, they had thrown up clouds of dust and a mushroomy scent that mingled with the smell of petrol leaking from the quad.

Robin saw no blood, so Lucy must have been wearing a decent helmet. But the tree had disintegrated and it was miraculous that she hadn't been knocked out. At the far side of the track a big clump of turf and a holly bush with a length of chain tied to its stump had been ripped out of the ground.

Chain traps were a common bandit tactic: find a tight corner on a forest track, stretch a chain or rope tightly across, and by the time a motorbike or quad rider sees the threat, they have no time to stop.

At the back of the quad, the big pink box had been squashed and its lid had flipped open, but Lucy had packed the cake for a bumpy ride, with three layers of bubble wrap. The iced lettering on top was legible through the wrapping, and Robin felt upset when he read the message:

Happy Naming Day, Zach William Maid

'William?' Robin gasped, practically inhaling his own tongue. 'What the . . . ?'

But baby Zach's name wasn't important while Lucy remained in danger.

He could hear the bandits in the trees less than ten metres away. Lucy was conscious and calm, using a bossy tone as she urged her captors to turn their lives around and join the rebels.

'Do you want to be part of the solution or part of the problem?' she challenged them. 'You'll be lucky to get thirty bucks for my shabby phone and silver rings. But us rebels need fit young people like you. You'll get regular food, hot showers and a private suite in the castle hotel.'

Robin crept close enough to see one bandit's outline. He wasn't far out of his teens, and Robin winced as he slapped Lucy with the back of his hand and growled nastily.

'Quit yapping and pull those rings off, you dirty hippy!' he demanded. 'Else I'll chop the fingers that go with 'em.'

'I haven't taken this off in years,' Lucy whimpered, tugging desperately at a silver skull ring. Robin eyed the crack in her purple safety helmet and the blood coming from a cut on the side of her neck.

It seemed there were three bandits: two stocky, dirt-caked youths and an older woman wrapped in a raggedy bearskin coat who held a shotgun.

Probably their mother, Robin guessed.

Robin reached over one shoulder, expertly hooked four of the arrows sticking out of his backpack between fingers, then swung them over his head. The first arrow notched into his bow, while the other three balanced in his hand, ready to shoot in rapid succession.

One for each bandit, and one for luck, Robin thought. Then realised he should take out the woman with the gun first.

2. THE RETURN OF ALAN ADALE

Robin Hood met Alan Adale by a nursery school sandbox when he was four years old, and they'd been mates ever since. While Robin and Josie bagged grass and listened to distant thunder, Alan was a few kilometres south in the eye of the storm.

As lightning crashed, Alan's gangly frame charged down the eighteenth hole of Locksley's Purple Pheasant Golf Club. He moved as fast as uncomfortable spiked shoes and the set of rattling golf clubs on his back would allow.

The rain had flattened Alan's giant afro, and he flicked hair out of his face as he leaped onto the wooden porch around the clubhouse and entered the men's locker room.

'Look at the state of that!' a half-dressed golfer said, chuckling at the sight of Alan's crazily tangled hair.

The wood-panelled locker room was crammed with two dozen golfers who'd run for cover when the threat of lightning forced them off the course. They made Alan not want to grow old, with their sweaty feet, knee braces and thick grey chest hair.

Alan was eager to escape, but as a golf caddy he only earned tips, so he stuck it out as bantering men stripped off wet golf gear and got ready to hit the bar. Finally, the sour-tempered player whose clubs Alan had spent three hours carrying came in from the storm. His name was Ken and his face was bright red, with rain streaking down his glasses.

'Ken's about to have a heart attack!' a golfer towelling his bald head teased. 'When did you last run that far, fat boy?'

'Just keep polishing that thick skull of yours,' Ken shot back.

Alan stood straighter and spoke to Ken politely. 'If you have a towel in your locker, I'd be happy to dry your clubs and golf bag.'

To Alan's relief, Ken shook his head.

'You're a good kid,' Ken said, then pulled a damp leather wallet from the back of his trousers and peeled off three twenty-pound notes.

Thirty was a normal tip for three hours carrying someone's golf clubs, forty was decent, and usually you only got more if the person you were caddying won his game and wanted to show off in front of his pals.

Ken had barely smiled all afternoon, so Alan was well pleased.

'That's very generous, sir.'

'Look at Ken flashing the cash,' the bald golfer shouted across the room.

Ken gave Alan a slap on the back, then held his arms out wide. 'This kid needs money for a haircut.'

Alan fake-smiled as golfers who were close enough to hear laughed at his expense. He couldn't bite back, because Locksley was a poor town and the Purple Pheasant Golf Club had a list of a hundred eager teens who'd snap up his caddying job if someone made a complaint.

'I'll consider a haircut,' Alan told Ken politely, then waved to the other golfers. 'Enjoy the rest of your weekend, sirs,' he told them.

Alan muttered, 'Gross, smelly, overprivileged old farts,' under his breath as he exited the gentlemen's locker room and dripped across a carpeted hallway. He grabbed the doorknob of a tatty store room where lowly caddies like him were allowed to change and leave their backpacks. But before he stepped in, a man shouted from the rowdy bar to his left.

'Hey, sonny boy! Get your hide in here.'

Alan cringed as he turned and saw his dad, Nick. He stood at a mahogany and marble bar next to his boss, Guy Gisborne.

'Mr Gisborne wants to say hello.' Nick beckoned. 'Let him see how tall you've grown!'

Like the changing room, the bar was rammed with golfers kicked off by the thunderstorm. The sign over the door said *Club Members Only* and Alan copped filthy looks as he pushed between tables. But all disapproval vanished once the golfers saw that the soggy caddy had been called to meet the gangster who ran every criminal racket in Locksley – and the police department that was supposed to stop him.

'Look at this boy, way up in the clouds!' Guy Gisborne teased. His eyes were nasty black marbles and his leather jacket creaked as he shook Alan's hand. 'Last time I saw you, you were about this high.'

Gisborne held his fingers ten centimetres apart, and Nick Adale laughed like his boss had told the funniest joke in history. Alan felt cringy, and longed to get into the caddies' room and out of his rain-soaked polo shirt. But his stomach drew his eyes towards calamari rings and pizzettas on the bar.

'Dig in!' Gisborne urged. 'Teen boys have always gotta eat!'

Alan waited for a nod from his dad before taking one of the mini pizzas.

'Gave your dad a big promotion a couple of months back,' Gisborne said, sounding full of himself. 'He's my troubleshooter. One of my top, top guys.'

Alan's mouth was stuffed, so he could only nod.

'So how come?' Gisborne continued, slurring because he was on his fifth drink. 'How come you are out caddying for tips with the scumbag kids from social housing? Don't I pay your daddy enough?'

Alan answered cheekily. 'My dad's mean, I guess.'

Gisborne roared with laughter. 'I *like* this kid.'

'I want my son and daughter to work and learn the value of money,' Nick explained, looking awkward. 'Not just have the good life handed down on a plate. Though I did put in a word with the club chairman to make sure Alan jumped the caddy waiting list.'

'Nothing wrong with honest graft,' Gisborne said, before his tone turned darker. 'And what about your bestie, Alan? Young Robin Hood? Have you heard from him lately?'

Alan almost inhaled a calamari ring. His dad was tight with Guy Gisborne, but the gangster was notorious for his temper and could have anyone beaten and thrown in jail if he chose to.

'Mr Gisborne,' Alan began, trying to sound serious, but not so much that it sounded fake. 'I've had no contact with Robin since he shot you in the . . . I mean, since he escaped into Sherwood Forest. I cooperated with Locksley police when they interviewed me. We even agreed to let them monitor my phone and social media accounts in case Robin ever tried to contact me.'

'Very good,' Gisborne said, but narrowed his eyes and cupped his chin, as if he wasn't sure he believed him.

Alan tried not to shudder. He still got occasional messages from Robin through an untraceable account on a gaming server, and Robin had turned up at his home one time to use his dad's 3D printer.

'If you ever get a sniff of Robin's whereabouts, make sure I'm the first to know,' Gisborne said. 'I'll see you're paid enough that you'll never need to carry another bag of golf clubs.'

'That's very kind,' Alan said, feeling queasy but hiding it well.

Brief silence indicated that Gisborne was done meeting Alan. Nick glanced at his watch before looking at his son. 'I'll be heading out of here in twenty minutes. You got dry clothes to change into?'

'Joggers and hoodie in my backpack,' Alan said.

'I'll give you a ride home and we'll drop by Wally's Steakhouse on the way,' Nick said. 'Mr Gisborne's restaurant just reopened after the roof got fixed.'

'Can't go wrong with a big steak,' Alan said keenly, then looked at Guy Gisborne as he backed away. 'Real pleasure to meet you again, Mr Gisborne.'

3. CALCULATED RISK

Robin stared down his arrow. He had a clean shot at the gun-toting bandit's chest. From this range, his arrow would likely pass through her torso and wind up embedded in the giant tree trunk behind.

The two youths would instinctively turn towards the person who'd been shot – like they always did. By the time they glanced back to see where the arrow had come from, they'd have one of Robin's arrows sticking in their thigh or their gut.

If I hit her through the heart, she'll die instantly, Robin thought.

If there had just been one bandit, Robin could have chanced something less lethal, like shooting the woman through her hand or knee. But she was less than three metres from Lucy and had her finger on the trigger of a shotgun that could kill or horribly wound her.

If I pop the bandit's lung, she'll suffocate.

If I miss her vital organs, she might survive if she can get to a hospital, but out here in the forest there's not much chance of that . . .

Robin wished it was like a movie, where the hero shoots a dozen people, there's no blood, and he runs off without giving a damn.

I really don't want to kill someone today.

Why did I have to be out here when this happened?

Robin found his fingers locked around the bow string. He couldn't let the arrow fly.

I'm losing my nerve. I'm turning chicken . . .

Or is this how you're supposed to feel when you're about to shoot a carbon-fibre arrow through the body of another human?

As Robin hesitated, Lucy kept trying to yank the silver skull ring off her middle finger. Then she wailed as one of the youths grabbed her wrist and began wrenching with such force that he lifted her off the ground.

'No!' Lucy begged, sobbing with pain as her finger crunched and dislocated.

She's suffering, Robin thought. *Can't let this go on . . .*

He shifted his aim towards the guy who was practically ripping Lucy's finger off, then aimed down towards his calf. The beefy youth howled as the arrow speared his Achilles tendon and came twenty centimetres out of the other side.

The youth let Lucy go and stumbled back, retching when he saw the arrow through his leg and the warm blood soaking his sock.

'I told you we were too far inside the compound!' the other youth shouted to the woman as he glanced around, apparently expecting to get jumped by a swarm of rebel guards.

Lucy did the right thing, burying her face in the undergrowth to avoid getting shot.

Robin had taken a risk by not shooting the woman who had the gun. Luckily, the guy he'd shot in the leg was thrashing about and the woman couldn't work out where Robin's arrow had come from. She pointed the big shotgun in several directions as she made rapid, breathless glances.

'Can you walk?' the uninjured youth gasped, trying to help the other guy up.

'Does it look like I can walk?' the guy with the arrow through his ankle blasted back, before howling in pain.

'Put your arm around my shoulders – we *have* to get out of here.'

Robin had his second arrow notched, and kept his aim on the woman with the gun. But instead of shooting her, he let the arrow skim through her furry bearskin hood and thud into the tree behind.

'Go, go, go!' the woman squealed, freaking out as Robin had hoped.

She ducked and scrambled around the back of the trunk.

'Leon can hardly walk,' the guy helping the injured bandit gasped.

If the woman was the victim's mother, as Robin suspected, she didn't show much maternal instinct.

'He's wrecked – ditch him!' she shouted, as she reached from behind the tree to grab her stuff. 'I'm outta here. That arrow nearly took my head off.'

As she lunged for her backpack, the uninjured youth gave a pitiful *I'm sorry* glance as he let his injured comrade drop back into the dirt.

'You can't abandon me!' Leon squealed. 'We go way back!'

As the uninjured youth ran after the woman, Robin closed on Lucy, who'd been slowly crawling towards him. Muddy and tearful, she groaned when she recognised Robin.

'Never thought I'd be this happy to see your ugly mug!' Lucy said.

She managed a relieved smile, despite red slap marks on her face, a cut on her neck and a dislocated finger.

'I've got to disarm the guy I shot,' Robin told her. 'I've got first aid in my backpack. I'll be back in a second.'

But before Robin moved off, he heard boots squelching along the muddy track.

'Quiet,' Robin told Lucy, putting a finger over his lips. 'It's probably our people, but stay low until I get eyes on them.'

While Robin crept back towards the track and ducked behind Lucy's wrecked quad bike, a commotion broke out among the trees where the two bandits had tried to escape. An instant later, Robin was relieved to see three rebel security officers sploshing mud as they ran down the boggy path. They were led by Lyla Masri, the Deputy Chief.

'Lyla!' Robin gasped, as he bobbed up above the quad. 'Over here.'

As Lyla rushed in and asked Robin to explain the situation, the second officer reached Lucy and unzipped a medical bag, while the third disarmed the teenage bandit with Robin's arrow speared through his ankle.

Moments later, two more security officers came out of the trees, marching the two bandits who'd tried to escape at gunpoint.

Robin almost felt sorry for the captives as the security team made them kneel in the mud and yanked zip ties tightly around their wrists. Neither their clothes nor their bodies had been washed in weeks. The woman had wrecked sneakers rather than waterproof hiking boots, and although the coldest months of winter had passed, their cheeks and hands bore patches of cracked red skin that indicated early frostbite.

'You know, anyone can come into Sherwood Castle and get a hot meal,' Lyla told the two cuffed bandits irritably, as her colleagues moved off to help carry the guy Robin shot. 'You might have to queue for a couple of hours, but isn't that better than trying to rip an innocent woman's finger off for a cheap ring?'

'Stick your do-gooder rebel charity,' the female bandit growled, as her flying spit spattered Lyla's black combat trousers. 'Who made you lot the law? Do you think you've got the right to lock people in dungeons now you've captured Sherwood Castle?'

Lyla felt frustrated enough to give the woman a taste of her boot, but acted professional, taking a deep breath and beginning an explanation.

'When us *do-gooders* take you back to the castle, you'll get hot food and a bath. We'll wash your clothes, we'll take your injured pal to the medical unit, and if you're lucky we might find some boots to replace those pathetic trainers.'

The woman snorted like she didn't believe a word, but Lyla finished her explanation.

'Once you're cleaned and fed, we'll take your photographs and a DNA sample. If you're not prepared to stay in this area and live by our rules, we'll put you in a truck and dump you a hundred kilometres west of here. *But* you better not cause trouble around here again, because I promise you this: No bandit will ever cause trouble a third time.'

Lucy was back on her feet, cheerful despite her injuries as she reached the path with a security officer supporting her.

'I was running *super* late because I spent ages putting extra bubble wrap around the cake for Zack's naming ceremony,' Lucy explained. 'Riding too fast. Should have slowed down. This tight corner is an obvious spot for a chain trap and I guess the quad bike is a total write-off . . .'

'Could have happened to any of us,' the guard holding Lucy's arm said sympathetically. 'Bandits are getting cocky, coming this close to the castle.'

'Will Scarlock is too soft, giving 'em a first warning,' another guard added. 'How long before one of us gets killed?'

Lucy cracked a smile when she saw Robin over by the wrecked quad. She dropped her escort and set off to give him a hug, but she only used one arm because of her bad finger.

'I was so scared when I couldn't get that stupid skull ring off,' Lucy explained, before planting a sweaty kiss on Robin's forehead. 'And clever shooting the guy in the leg so nobody got badly hurt.'

Lyla gave Robin a fierce scowl when she heard this. 'I train security teams to always aim at the biggest target, same way the cops and the army do. The only place I want to see someone take a risky trick shot is in a movie.'

Robin let Lyla's warning roll over him and spoke to Lucy. 'The cake you made seems OK. A few cracks in the icing, but amazing considering it was tied to a quad bike that flipped and demolished a rotting tree.'

'I used enough bubble wrap to withstand a nuclear blast,' Lucy joked.

Robin smiled, then stared awkwardly at the mud between his boots before feeling brave enough to ask the question that was burning his insides.

'I saw the name you wrote in the icing,' Robin said weakly. 'Zach *William* Maid.'

'Ahh,' Lucy said awkwardly. 'Did Karma and Indio discuss that?'

Robin looked sour and shook his head. 'I thought it was Zach *Robin* Maid. They said he was being named after me.'

Lyla gave orders as a little Sherwood Castle Resort branded SUV closed in. 'We need to clear this area and sweep for more bandits,' she began. 'I want Robin, Lucy and the three captives out of here.'

Lucy hoped Lyla's interruption would get her out of Robin's awkward questioning. But he'd just rescued her and she knew he deserved an answer.

'Robin . . .' Lucy began, then paused for a big sigh. 'Indio and Karma have had a *really* stressful time lately . . . You know, with a huge family to look after and a new baby and . . .'

Robin squinted and gritted his teeth because he didn't want to sound upset. 'They don't want to name their baby after me now because they think it's my fault their daughter Marion got caught.'

'It's not quite as simple as that,' Lucy said. 'They decided to use William as the middle name, after Will Scarlock.'

Robin thought it was a weak excuse, but the little Suzuki SUV had pulled up and it felt wrong to argue with Lucy when she was injured. Since he was the smallest, Robin had to squat on a spare tyre in the trunk. He gagged at the stench of the three filthy, handcuffed bandits squashed up on the back seat.

Loud moans from the guy with the arrow through his ankle didn't stop Robin feeling sorry for himself as the Suzuki made the short drive back to the castle.

Everyone blames me for Marion getting busted.

Indio and Karma are wanted criminals, so they can't visit her.

Marion will be twenty when she gets out of Pelican Island. It's not fair that they blame me.

If I'd been more careful, Marion wouldn't have got caught.

Why didn't I look around to make sure Marion was in the other car before we drove away?

4. CADDY SHACK

Alan shuddered, thinking about his encounter with Guy Gisborne. A thug who kept a rhino skin Sjambok whip in his car and was known to pull out his smartphone and show off videos of the people he'd used it on.

The tatty store room where golf caddies changed had emptied out by the time Alan arrived, although they'd left clumps of mud and whiffs of body spray behind. His rain-soaked polo shirt made a satisfying slap as it hit the floor. He put on a dry tracksuit top and dug a hairband out of his rucksack to keep his soggy hair off his face.

As Alan slid his feet into Nikes, a wood-panelled door at the opposite end of the storage room clicked open. He barely saw the two people who entered because his view was blocked by towers of stacking chairs and the fold-up tables used at the club's formal dinners.

'Told you we'd get privacy in here,' a bulky figure said, as he entered ahead of a woman in her late teens. 'The caddies rushed off to catch the four-fifteen bus.'

'Perfect make-out spot,' the girl answered dryly. 'Can't beat smells of armpits and floor polish.'

Alan froze, sure he knew both voices from somewhere as the girl backed into the stacked tables and let the boy kiss her. He decided to sneak out and leave them to it, but as he picked up his backpack his sneaker squeaked on the damp floor.

'Sorry, I'm heading out,' Alan blurted, snatching his hoodie off a hook and lunging for the main door.

'Alan!' the guy on the other side of the stacking chairs said curiously. 'Is that you?'

Alan placed the voice as he turned and saw the enormous frame of Robin Hood's brother, Little John.

'It's been a while!' Alan said, as Little John squeezed between two towers of chairs, followed by his girlfriend, Clare Gisborne.

Alan had visited Robin's house hundreds of times while he was growing up. Little John was four years older and always tried to stay out of their way.

But while John was a shy giant, Clare Gisborne had been Locksley High School's number-one bully. She'd been obsessed with proving she was better at soccer than any boy, and was an expert kick-boxer who wanted everyone to think she was as mean and nasty as her father, Guy.

'Good to see you, Alan,' Little John said, better dressed and more confident than the kid Alan remembered.

Alan found it weird that Clare was now John's girlfriend. She still packed enough muscle to flip Alan like a pancake, but she seemed to have outgrown her permanent scowl and her habit of copying her dad's all-black wardrobe.

'I saw you two on telly at the election rally,' Alan said. 'I hear you're both boarders at Barnsdale School now.'

'We went from enemies to frenemies, to boyfriend and girlfriend in one term,' John said, making Clare laugh.

Alan realised he'd never heard Clare laugh before. Or rather, he'd never heard her laugh like a normal person, instead of the mad cackle that would erupt when she threw a kid over a balcony, or ordered one of her minions to dunk someone's head in a toilet bowl.

'Do you two golf?' Alan asked.

Clare and Little John shuddered at the thought.

'Golf is *so* boring!' Clare said. 'My dad held a fundraising lunch for his election campaign here earlier, so I had to dress up nice and be the good daughter.'

'Raising money Guy Gisborne style,' John added. 'Any guest who donates less than two thousand pounds takes a one-way dive off Main Street Bridge.'

Alan laughed, but Clare looked annoyed at the insult to her family.

'Your mum, Sheriff Marjorie, is no saint.' Clare smouldered.

John swiftly changed the subject. 'Ever hear from my little brother?' he asked.

'Robin? Never,' Alan answered, wary of Clare and the threat her father had made. 'You?'

John nodded. 'Robin has to change contact details all the time to prevent surveillance, but we manage to chat. I can put you in touch. I'm sure he'd love to hear from you.'

Clare noticed Alan's unease. 'I stay out of the beef between my dad and Robin,' she told him. 'I'd lose my sanity if I didn't.'

Alan wasn't sure what to believe. 'Your dad doesn't mind you dating Robin Hood's brother?'

Clare smirked and looked up at Little John. 'John is Robin Hood's big brother,' she agreed. 'But his mum is Sheriff Marjorie, and since she's hot favourite to become our next president, my dad won't risk upsetting her.'

'How's Robin doing?' Alan asked.

'Almost too quiet,' John answered. 'No raids or robberies, and he's really into this Josie chick.'

Clare thumped John's arm.

'What was that for?'

'Women are *not* chicks,' Clare said firmly. 'Misogynist pig.'

'Last summer, clips of Robin were getting millions of views and half the kids in the country had *Robin Hood Lives* T-shirts,' Alan noted. 'Now I guess they've moved on to the next big thing.'

John nodded. 'I'm all for Robin living the quiet life if it means he's safe and happy.'

'And your dad, Ardagh?' Alan asked. 'I heard he's got an appeal coming up.'

John nodded. 'He's got this whip-smart lawyer, Tybalt Bull, on the case. The cops who accused my dad of assault filed the wrong paperwork, so there's a chance his prison sentence for assaulting them will be overturned. The bad news is, it could be months before my dad's appeal gets heard by a judge.'

'It'd be good to see Ardagh out of prison,' Alan said fondly. 'Your dad never spoke much when I visited your house, but when he did it was always interesting.'

Before Alan could say more, the main door of the caddies' locker room opened and his father leaned in, tapping the face of his watch.

'You're worse than your ma, the time it takes you to get changed,' Nick complained. 'The valet's bringing my car to the front entrance and I've got a bunch of calls to make for Mr Gisborne when we get home, so step up the pace and let's get out of here.'

5. CHOCOLATE CREAM

'You don't have much to be grumpy about,' Josie told Robin.

She'd showered and put on clean leggings and a smart top for the naming ceremony. Now she was in Robin's bedroom in the Sherwood Castle penthouse. Robin stood bare-chested in front of a mirrored wardrobe, pleased with how muscly he looked, annoyed at how short he was, and unable to decide between his two smartest shirts.

'The one with the curry stain, or the one with three missing buttons?' he asked.

Josie snorted as she crashed backwards onto Robin's giant bed and kicked her feet in the air. 'Your sartorial elegance knows no bounds,' she answered airily. 'I *told* you to buy that shirt at the Wednesday market.'

Robin huffed. 'And who says I'm grumpy?'

'You're always moaning!' Josie said, as she rolled over and hugged a corner of Robin's duvet. 'You've got it good here. A giant bed in a penthouse. Karma and Indio make wicked food. Matt and Otto worship the ground you walk on, you've got loads of money, and the cutest girl in Sherwood Castle is your girlfriend.'

'You're too modest.' Robin laughed, then turned serious. 'I *know* I'm well looked after, Josie. I know there are kids in the forest who drink river water and sleep under plastic tarps. But right now, it's just uncomfortable . . .'

'Uncomfortable how?'

'Karma and Indio. Ever since Marion got busted, I don't think they like me.'

Josie sat up. 'Well, what do you expect? They ordered you and Marion to come home after you freed the hackers in the forest. You ignored them, you staged a crazy robbery, and Marion got mashed up by cops and thrown in jail.'

Robin groaned as he slipped the curry-stained shirt up his arms. 'But Marion's independent. I didn't force her to do anything. And this thing today, changing baby Zack's name and not mentioning it proves they're pissed off with me. I bet they'd kick me out of this penthouse if it didn't make them look bad.'

'Life's not black and white,' Josie said. 'Indio and Karma still care about you. But you also remind them that they've got a daughter in prison. It's not *totally* your fault that Marion got busted, but she didn't go off doing robberies before you turned up.'

'I wish that night never happened,' Robin said as he struggled to do up his top buttons.

'Shirt's too small,' Josie said, bursting into laughter. 'You look ridiculous.'

'I guess I'm too muscular and buff for my own damned clothes,' Robin said, flexing his biceps and hoping he'd rip the shirt like the Incredible Hulk.

'You'll have to go to the naming ceremony in one of your plaid shirts,' Josie said. 'Hopefully there's one that isn't three weeks unwashed and splattered with chicken poop.'

'The lumberjack look.' Robin sighed as Marion's eight-year-old brother Otto charged dramatically into the room. He wore a shirt, a giant tie, one sock and Mario Kart briefs.

'Mummy Indio wants to see you,' Otto told Robin.

Otto was a terrible liar, and his smirk and excited eyes made Robin suspicious.

'Oh, really?' Robin asked. 'What for?'

'How should I know?' Otto groaned theatrically. 'She needs you *now*.'

At the same time Karma shouted from out in the hallway. 'The naming ceremony starts in twenty-five minutes. You kids had better all be out of the shower and getting your clothes on.'

'If you're pranking me, I'll kick your butt,' Robin warned Otto, tugging the undersized shirt over his head and stepping into the hallway. As Robin exited his bedroom, ten-year-old Matt Maid sprang from behind the door, holding a can of chocolate-flavoured spray cream and shooting it in Robin's face.

'Idiot!' Robin gasped, coughing and inhaling cream. 'I'm . . . getting ready.'

Robin spun back towards his room, in time to see Josie pull two cans of cream from under his bed and throw one to Otto. As Otto and Matt shot cream in Robin's face and down his back, Josie grabbed the elastic on the back of Robin's undershorts and aimed down his crack.

'It's freezing!' Robin yelped as he hopped around his room trying to escape. Then he spun around and pointed at Josie. 'You set the boys up to do this!'

'What, little old me?' Josie said, feigning innocence as Robin tried to escape into his bathroom. But Matt blocked his way and Josie knocked Robin sideways with a well-aimed pillow that sent him stumbling into an armchair.

'Robin looks like he crapped his pants!' Otto sang cheerfully, before feeding himself with a generous squirt from his can of chocolate cream. 'Robin crapped his paaaaaants!'

'Bog off.' Robin squirmed as Josie took her phone off the bed and started snapping photos.

'These are going on every social network unless you're *very* nice to me,' Josie threatened.

'There's cream all over my floor,' Robin protested, skidding on the marble floor as blobs of chocolate cream slid down his legs like slugs. 'I'm not cleaning this up.'

'This is gold!' Matt laughed cheerfully, while letting his empty can of cream drop in a bin.

Now the shock attack was over, Robin saw himself in the mirror. He started to laugh, then scooped a big blob of cream off his chest and squished it through his hair like styling mousse.

'I hate all three of you!' Robin said. 'I've just had a shower, now I'll have to go again. And I'll have to wash my bedsheets.'

'First time for everything,' Josie said. 'You do know duvet covers are supposed to bend?'

Otto and Matt's smiles disappeared as Karma stepped into the doorway, attracted by all the noise.

'For crying out loud!' she thundered, though she couldn't completely disguise a smile.

'It wasn't me, I just got here!' Otto lied.

Otto had kicked his empty can under Robin's bed, but the ring of chocolate cream around his mouth exposed the lie.

'Otto, go to your room, wipe your face and put your smart trousers on,' Karma ordered. 'Matt, get the mop from the kitchen and wipe this floor before the cream treads everywhere. Robin, shower *quickly*. Josie, you can stay out of mischief by helping Indio and me carry the trays of food down to the ground floor.'

'Why do I have to clean up?' Matt protested.

Karma poked Matt in the chest and looked furious. 'Because I said so, buster. And the next kid who backchats me will be loading the dishwasher after breakfast and dinner every day for the next month! So, get cracking before I *really* lose my temper.'

The four kids decided to do what they were told, but once the others were out of Robin's room Karma spoke more gently as he stepped into his bathroom.

'Did you see the new shirt I hung in your wardrobe?'

'Eh?' Robin asked.

'You only had one decent shirt, and the buttons popped off when you wore it on Christmas Day,' Karma explained. 'So I bought that striped one you liked.'

'Nice!' Robin said, as he slid his wardrobe door open to check it out. 'I didn't see it was there. Thank you.'

'Gotta look smart for Zach's ceremony,' Karma said. 'Speaking of which, I've got to go and beautify myself.'

As Matt came back with a wet mop, Robin closed his bathroom door, hung his new shirt on the door and stared at it thoughtfully. He realised Josie was right about Indio and Karma. They blamed him for Marion getting caught, and it had complicated their feelings towards him. But they hadn't stopped caring about him.

6. SWEET LITTLE LIES

Alan stared at the sun setting over central Locksley's abandoned office buildings as he rode in the front passenger seat of his dad's plush Mercedes. They were going twenty kilometres an hour over the limit but, as one of Guy Gisborne's top guys, Nick Adale wouldn't get a speeding ticket.

The ten months since Robin escaped into the forest had been the weirdest of Alan's life. His mum, Nasha, had left. She'd been the boss of Locksley Transport Department, but moved away when she landed her dream job running the Capital City Metro system.

But the job was only part of the story. As months passed, Alan and his sister Dakota found out that his parents hadn't told the whole truth. Besides the metro job and swanky Capital City apartment, his mum had a boyfriend – and Alan had seen letters from a divorce lawyer.

On the rare occasions when Alan's mum called, she'd hang up after a few awkward minutes. Visits to

Capital City in the school holidays kept getting called off, because his mum was sick or she had some vital report to prepare.

Meanwhile, Alan's dad got his own promotion. Nick threw himself into being Guy Gisborne's troubleshooter and splashed money around like water. Watches, suits, custom golf clubs, the new Mercedes. Even a speedboat at Skegness Island that he'd never taken out of its mooring.

'Did you earn a decent tip today?' Nick asked as he shot through an intersection where the traffic lights hadn't worked in years.

'Sixty,' Alan answered grumpily.

'Decent for three hours' graft,' Nick said. 'My first job paid three twenty an hour, mopping floors at Mindy Burger.'

Alan couldn't think how to answer, so he grunted.

It wasn't like he didn't speak to his dad, but it was only about stuff like groceries, the weather and homework. If Alan asked what was going on with the divorce, asked if his mum was OK, or mentioned that he'd heard Dakota crying in her room, his dad always brushed it off with a bland platitude:

We'll get through it.

Time is the great healer.

Your mother loves you, but she needs space right now.

'We'll ask for our steaks and starters to come together,' Nick said. 'I want to get out of Wally's before Gisborne shows up. I've got paperwork and phone calls, and if

Gisborne arrives in the mood to party, I won't get home till sunrise.'

'What about Dakota?' Alan asked. 'Aren't we picking her up for dinner?'

Nick shook his head. 'She's sleeping over.'

Alan tutted. 'Dad, she slept over *last* night. Dakota played rugby this afternoon and Susie's mum said she'd look after her until you got back from golf.'

'Really?' Nick said, smashing a palm on the steering wheel and speeding up. 'So, we'll go fetch her first.'

There was little traffic on the broad avenues through central Locksley, but Nick had downed several scotches at the golf club and these streets had potholes big enough to crack a wheel.

'Dad, slow down!' Alan warned.

Nick ignored his son. 'Get Susie's mum's address,' he snapped. 'It's in the satnav.'

'Maybe we should go to Wally's tomorrow,' Alan suggested. 'Pick up Dakota, get fish and chips on the way home and have a quiet evening.'

'I promised Gisborne we'd check Wally's out now it's reopened,' Nick said, while his son scrolled through the car's navigation screen looking for Susie's address. 'Better go tonight, because it doesn't take much for Gisborne to take offence.'

'Dakota doesn't like steak,' Alan pointed out as the car clanked over a loose manhole cover. 'Do they have a kids' menu?'

'In two hundred and fifty metres, turn right. Then take the second exit onto Junction Road,' the satnav announced.

To Alan's relief, the turn into an alleyway forced his dad to slow down. As they drove past a burnt-out parking garage, Nick's phone rang and Guy Gisborne's name appeared on the car's main display console.

'Your boyfriend,' Alan said, then blew a sarcastic kiss.

'Quiet,' Nick said. All the veins in his neck bulged as he answered the call and put it on speaker. 'Hey, boss, what can I do you for?'

Guy Gisborne sounded stressed. 'Got a situation at the Mile End Landfill, Zone J. Bunch of idiots clearing a blocked pipe hit a gas pocket and blew themselves up. I'm sending some muscle down to clean up and make sure the press don't stick their noses in, but I need someone with a brain to take charge of the situation.'

'Where's Kendall?' Nick asked. 'She runs waste management.'

'I know she does,' Gisborne roared nastily. 'But she's not answering her phone and I can't risk showing my face at the scene of an industrial accident when I'm running for Sheriff. That leaves you as my problem-solving guy to solve a problem, like I pay you to.'

'Absolutely, boss,' Nick said, pulling up to the kerb then looking over his shoulder to make a U-turn. 'It's across town, but I'll be there in twenty.'

7. ENVIRONMENTAL EXCELLENCE

Guy Gisborne started his criminal career dealing drugs and forcing local business owners to pay him protection money. Then, like many ambitious criminals before him, Gisborne discovered there was money to be made in trash.

When any of Capital City's ten million citizens tossed a bag of rubbish, it got loaded onto a truck or river barge and ended up in one of several vast landfill sites that Guy Gisborne owned around Locksley.

Tough rules on recycling and protecting the environment make it hard for waste disposal companies to make an *honest* profit. But crooks can make millions by ignoring the regulations and paying off the government inspectors who are supposed to enforce them.

Alan's first impression of the Mile End landfill site was of a slick operation. His dad's Mercedes skimmed down a smooth tarmac road, past more than a kilometre of neat green fencing, with LED floodlights and yellow *Keep Out* signs.

After the luxurious car overtook twenty rubbish trucks queuing back from the site's main entrance, Nick Adale stopped in front of a portable office building with a huge *Gisborne Waste Management* sign on top. The slogan beneath read *Leading the way in recycling and environmental excellence.*

As Alan watched a rubbish cart reverse into a marked bay and tip its load down a giant metal chute, a woman in a reflective orange overall rushed from the hut towards the Mercedes.

Alan gagged at the stench of trash as his dad lowered the window.

The woman gave a complex set of directions, which Nick struggled to follow. They took a left and kept driving past the never-ending fence. After a while, the tarmac became a narrow gravel track with no lights, and stones plinking the underside of the car.

Zone J had no signpost. Nick missed an unmarked break in the fence and had to back up. After a hundred metres, the steep single-lane track opened into a large gravel oval, with metal railings circling the edge and a vista across the entire landfill.

They were atop the oldest part of the site, where the mountain of trash had been stacked high, then capped with several metres of topsoil and planted with grass.

The area that was currently being filled was visible to Alan's left, with long conveyor belts collecting trash dumped by the trucks. Bulldozers with solid metal wheels levelled the rubbish, while workers in filthy orange overalls used sprinkler hoses to tamp down the dust and stink.

Directly ahead, cars streaked along a busy highway, and beyond the traffic another vast hole was being dug, big enough for Mile End Landfill to gobble Capital City trash for years to come.

Nick parked up near two battered green vans with flashing orange lights and the Gisborne Waste Management logo. Two guys stood, their hands buried in the pockets of their dirty orange overalls, while a woman slumped against the side of one van. Alan was alarmed when the Mercedes' headlamps lit her up, showing blood down one side of her face and her orange overall turned to strings of melted plastic.

'Dad, what happened?' Alan gulped.

A powerful stench of rubbish and smoke filled the car as his dad jumped out. 'Stay where you are,' Nick ordered.

'That woman's burned,' Alan said urgently. 'Why aren't those guys helping her?'

'Don't speak to anyone,' was all Nick added, before he slammed the car door.

Alan was plunged into darkness as his dad shut off the Mercedes' lights. Nick said something to the two guys in overalls before jogging off with them down a stepped footpath and out of sight.

The stench of burnt trash stuck in the back of Alan's throat, so he reached across to take a bottle of water from the pocket in the driver's side door.

It felt creepy sitting in the dark, knowing the horribly injured woman was less than twenty metres away. There was little moonlight and an eerie soundscape came out of the dark: noisy gulls pecking at the trash, the rumble of giant bulldozers, and distant clanks as the endless stream of trash carts dropped their loads.

'Should have taken the bus home.' Alan sighed to himself.

He slid his phone out and tried not to think about what was going on. He had no data signal, so he opened up a racing game that he hadn't played for weeks. Before completing a lap, Alan was jolted by a hollow metallic thump. He thought one of the giant gulls from the trash mound had landed on the car, but glanced up and saw the bloody-faced woman slumped over the hood of the car.

'Help,' she croaked, looking like something out of a horror movie, with a bloody face and her orange suit melted away to expose burned skin on her right shoulder. 'Please.'

Alan had orders to stay in the car, but he could hardly ignore her. He felt scared as he opened the door and stepped into the cold, vile-smelling air.

'Drive me to hospital,' the woman begged, her face contorted with pain.

'I'm thirteen,' Alan said. 'My dad has the keys.'

The woman lost her footing and splayed noisily across the hood of the car. Alan thought she was going to roll off and crash onto the gravel, but she held on by grasping the door mirror with a bloody hand.

'It's a cover-up,' the woman begged. 'They're going to kill me.'

'I've got no signal here,' Alan answered. 'They *must* have called an ambulance for you.'

Alan felt sick. The woman was struggling to breathe and every word strained her burned face.

'I'm an illegal,' the woman said. 'They'll bury me under the trash with the two who didn't come out.'

'Don't be daft,' Alan said, shaking his head in denial. 'My dad is in charge. He's a decent man. Let me help you sit down before you slip and hurt yourself.'

'I'm dead,' she repeated. 'Dead if you don't help me.'

8. HEIRANI STONE

'My dad will be back soon,' Alan repeated soothingly, while supporting the woman's arm on the side that wasn't burned. 'The ambulance will be here soon.'

But Alan had doubts as he slid the woman off the car, lowering her to the gravel with her back propped against the front tyre. His dad had taken half an hour to drive here from the centre of town, but the ambulance station at Locksley General was closer. And he remembered how the two men had stood around ignoring this poor woman when they arrived . . .

'Ambulance might take a while if they're busy,' Alan told her. 'Do you want some water?'

'There is no ambulance,' the woman insisted, as she gripped Alan's leg. 'They're sending us down there to vent gas, but it's too much. Too dangerous.'

Alan saw a pair of headlights coming up the track towards the oval clearing.

'Might be the ambulance,' he said hopefully.

But it was an ancient Honda saloon car, sagging from the weight of the four huge men squashed inside. As they climbed out wearing black gloves and ski masks, the woman looked at Alan with pleading eyes.

'Remember my name,' she croaked. 'Heirani Stone.'

'Boy, get on your knees,' a huge muscular man shouted as he blazed a torch in Alan's face.

Alan was so startled that he froze.

'Are you stupid, deaf, or both?' the man demanded, as he stepped up and booted Alan's feet away.

The giant caught Alan by the back of his hoodie as he fell, then slammed him hard into the side of his father's car.

'I'm . . .' Alan began, but the guy thumped him in the back and winded him.

As Alan crumpled against the car door, fighting for breath, two more thugs from the car grabbed Heirani.

'She's hurt,' Alan shouted.

'Show me your ID,' the guy looming over Alan demanded. 'You're not in an orange suit, so who are you? Why are you here?'

Heirani screamed as the two men picked her easily off the ground and dragged her towards the little car. One opened the trunk and squashed her in; the other pulled a rag out of his pocket and stuffed it in her mouth.

Alan was in pain, but finally got some air back in his lungs. 'Please speak to my dad,' he gasped, tasting blood from his split lip. 'Don't hurt her.'

The thug squashed Alan's cheeks out of shape with one massive hand.

'Who might your daddy be?' he growled.

'Nick Adale.'

The thug backed up like he'd received an electric shock, then eyed Alan suspiciously. 'Why'd Nick bring you up here?'

'We were driving to Wally's Steakhouse when Guy Gisborne called my dad and told him to come here.'

'Nicky's boy, eh?' the thug said, sounding really worried. 'I'm sorry I belted you. I thought you were forest scum, with the girl.'

Alan was relieved that the monster had stopped hurting him, but horrified to see the Honda's trunk slam down with Heirani inside.

'I'm sure this is all a mix-up,' Alan said desperately. 'Don't take her anywhere until my dad gets back.'

It seemed like they'd listened, because the guy standing by Alan ordered one of the others to go down the path and find Mr Adale. He came back a couple of minutes later, with Nick out of breath and one of the orange-suited landfill site employees.

'Dad,' Alan blurted, as he rushed over, pointing at the Honda. 'They put the woman in the trunk of that car.'

Nick scowled at his son. 'Keep your eyes down and your mouth shut,' he snapped. 'I *told* you to stay in the car.'

'She walked over here, Dad. She's burned. She was crying.'

Nick ignored his son and gave orders to the thugs. 'Carry the other two bodies up here, then hose that whole area with bleach. I need to pick up my daughter and get home.'

'Dad, what the heck!' Alan gasped, jaw hanging open.

Nick narrowed his eyes and tutted. 'Don't be a brat, Alan. You know who I work for.'

As Nick walked around to get in the driver's seat, he noticed Heirani's blood smeared on the hood and where her hand had grasped the door mirror.

'You got the wet golf shirt?' Nick asked. 'From earlier?'

Alan's hands trembled as he reached in the car and got the shirt out of his backpack. He'd always known his dad worked for Gisborne, but not that he did hands-on stuff like this . . .

As Nick used the wet shirt to wipe Heirani's blood away, Alan noticed that she'd dropped a little plastic card wallet as they dragged her off. After checking nobody was looking, he picked it up and dropped it in his backpack.

'Burn this with everything else,' Nick said, as he flung the bloody golf shirt towards one of the masked thugs.

Nick looked at his gawping son as they settled in the car and clicked on their seatbelts.

'I'll buy you a new shirt,' he said, as he started the engine. 'And this stays between us, you hear? Not a word to your little sister.'

9. THAT AWKWARD AGE

Robin could think of better ways to spend Saturday afternoon than sitting in an uncomfortable fold-out chair watching the naming ceremony for Zack Maid and two other rebel babies.

Will Scarlock gave a speech. Parents got tearful while a hairy bloke sang John Lennon's 'Give Peace a Chance', and random people earned polite applause for reading cheesy poems full of words like *love, hugs, rejoice* and *encouragement*. The only good bit was when Zack projectile-vomited on the official photographer.

The aftermath of the ceremony wasn't thrilling either. There was a long table stacked with food. Robin ate heaps, but suffered the awkwardness of being thirteen years old: too old to play tag and sock slide with little kids, too young to drink wine and gossip with grown-ups.

Josie had to go back to her room for a weekly call with her relatives in Albania, so Robin sat alone. He was considering sneaking back upstairs to his room when he noticed Indio talking to her sister, Lucy, a few metres away.

'Are they cutting the cake soon?' Robin asked, raising his voice over the function room's chatter.

Lucy had a foam neck brace and two fingers splinted together. It was miraculous that her injuries were so light after ripping the front axle off her quad bike and disintegrating a rotting tree stump.

As Robin stood up and stepped nearer, he saw that Indio was crying. But they'd both heard his question about the cake, so it was too late to back off.

'What's the matter?' Robin asked.

Indio shot Robin a fierce glare, then half smiled as she wiped her face with a party napkin.

'It's nothing, Robin,' she said, waving him off with one hand.

Robin didn't know what to say, but felt weird saying nothing.

'It's just . . .' he began awkwardly. 'Josie left with her dad and I'm sitting around. I thought I'd go up to the penthouse and chill . . . But I'll wait if they're cutting Zack's cake soon.'

Lucy backed away from her sister and gave Robin a *come with me* gesture.

'If you're bored, you can start filling black bags with rubbish and take them across to the trash compactor.'

So dumb, Robin told himself. *Why didn't I tell them I had homework to do?*

Cleaning up wasn't Robin's idea of fun, but he didn't make a fuss as Lucy pointed out a roll of black rubbish sacks on a window ledge.

'I know where to take it,' Robin said, stopping to let two little girls chase in front of him, and wondering why Lucy kept following him.

Lucy glanced over her shoulder to make sure Indio wasn't watching before speaking quietly.

'Indio got a message from Marion's dad, Cut-Throat. Marion's been having trouble with some older girls in her cell block at Pelican Island. She got shoved down a flight of stairs and she's in the medical unit.'

'Oh no!' Robin gasped, feeling like he'd been kicked in the gut as his inner voice reminded him that Marion being locked up was partly his fault. 'Did she break a bone?'

'We don't know. Cut-Throat only found out because one of the bikers from his gang is doing time at Pelican Island and has a job in the medical unit.'

Robin sighed. 'I thought Marion would be OK. The bikers have looked after my dad for the past year.'

Lucy shrugged. 'There are lots of bikers in the men's prison, but none with Marion in the teen girls' unit.'

'Never thought of that,' Robin admitted. 'And I heard that Marion's cousin, Freya Tuck, is on a different floor of the unit, so she can't stick up for her either.'

Lucy sighed. 'Indio and Karma are both upset, but they're keeping the news to themselves because they don't want to spoil this celebration for everyone else.'

'You better go back over to Indio,' Robin said. 'She looks wrecked.'

'Indio and Karma are both wanted by the cops, so they can't even visit Marion,' Lucy said. 'I'm trying to get on the visitors list so I can go see Marion, but I'm only her aunt and the paperwork takes weeks if you're not a parent.'

Robin felt angry enough to kick something, but instead he grabbed the roll of black bags and threw his anger into gathering empty beer cans and scraping plates. When he had a big bag of litter and two clanking sacks of cans, Robin headed out through the swinging back door of the function room and into a scruffy service corridor.

A bunch of kids, including Marion's brothers Otto and Finn, had escaped out here to bat party balloons and frisbee paper plates. A girl of about six excitedly asked Robin if he wanted to play, but he was in a mood and snapped at her.

'These bags are heavy – get out of my way!'

Before it became the rebel headquarters, Sherwood Castle was a sprawling hotel, resort and conference centre. All of the ground-floor food outlets and function rooms were connected by service corridors, and Robin waddled several hundred metres with the heavy bags before reaching a double-height room dominated by a pair of giant trash compactors.

Robin tipped the two bags of cans into a giant steel drawer, then pulled down a thick metal safety shield to activate the hydraulic crusher. After some pings and

50

clanks, the crusher popped open and revealed all the cans squashed into a neat cube.

He would normally have found this satisfying, but Robin felt angry and helpless when he thought about Marion getting bullied. As he walked across to a giant wheeled bin to dump the non-recyclable stuff, his phone vibrated in his back pocket.

Robin's hands were covered in stuff he'd scraped off plates, so he wiped them down the front of his trousers before checking the screen.

With a bounty on his head, Robin was wary about bad guys locating him through his phone. In theory, any message that reached his phone had been bounced around the world using a virtual private network and some sophisticated ghosting software installed by his hacking guru, D'Angela. But Robin was still suspicious of any message from a source he didn't recognise.

'Who's this?' Robin asked himself, as his screen showed a cryptic balloon notification from a gaming server.

After a moment he remembered it was the online tank battle game that he used to play with Alan back in primary school days. There was a green mouth icon to show that the person trying to contact him was waiting in a chat room.

'Alan, mate!' Robin said, cheered by the thought of a conversation with his oldest friend.

But Alan sounded desperate and could barely get his words out.

'I saw . . .' Alan said, then snorted back tears. 'My whole world . . .'

Robin felt shocked and anxious hearing his friend in such a state, but tried to stay calm. 'Mate, I know you're upset, but I can't understand what you're saying. Take a couple of deep breaths. Then speak slowly.'

'I saw them take this woman,' Alan said, as he tried not to sniffle. 'My dad was in charge and he didn't lift a finger. I see her face every time I close my eyes, and it makes me want to puke. I feel like my whole world has been turned upside down. I think . . . I mean, you've *always* been my best friend.'

'Sounds bad, mate,' Robin said soothingly, as he found a broken plastic bucket chair and dragged it to a spot where he could sit down. 'I'm here for you.'

'I'm not sure what to do, Robin. But maybe you guys can help me . . .'

10. PASSING GAS

Sherwood Castle was Sunday-morning quiet as Robin walked down from the twelfth-floor penthouse, then passed banks of dead slot machines in the abandoned casino. After crossing two hundred metres of garish carpet, he opened a door hidden behind a curtain and walked up a flight of steps into the space known as the Nest.

It had been built as a surveillance room for the casino, where security guards watched every machine and gaming table, on the lookout for cheating gamblers and thieving staff. Now the space was fitted out with a world-class hacking and surveillance system, left behind after a hostage rescue operation run by Robin's hacking guru, D'Angela Doncastro.

Robin had no idea where D'Angela and her hacking crew had gone after they left the forest, but she responded to messages whenever he had a problem and still sent him weekly hacking lessons and puzzles.

Thanks to this mentorship, Robin had progressed from a script kiddie, who copied ideas and only used hacks created by others, to someone with enough skills to write code and create simple hacking tools of his own.

The beating heart of the Nest was the Super, a frog-green supercomputer powered by racks of GPUs and blasted from all sides with cooling fans. In the hands of an expert operator, the Super's data lake software used artificial intelligence to sift through hundreds of databases and identify patterns.

The Super was linked to enough legal and illegal data sources to track most citizens from their birth certificate to their current mobile phone contract. If you got lucky, there might even be a CCTV image from the café where they drank their morning coffee.

Robin had only mastered a fraction of the powerful system's tools, but after much cursing and a lot of help from D'Angela he'd written a script that used data from spy satellites, mobile phones and walkie-talkies and a dozen direction-finding microphones spread across the castle roof to track bandit activity in the area around Sherwood Castle.

The software overlaid daily results onto a map. In the past twenty-four hours it showed fourteen suspicious incursions onto the castle's vast grounds, and when Robin used a slider to compare maps from the past, it was clear that the number of bandits in the area was growing and that they were getting bolder and operating closer to the castle.

Robin highlighted three areas on the map where it looked like bandits had been camping overnight, then sent the image across to rebel security chief Azeem Masri. She didn't have enough security people to deal with every bandit, but thanks to the Super a couple of the biggest threats would be flushed out of Sherwood Castle grounds before they could cause any more trouble.

After answering a couple of routine messages and a call from the security office asking for more details on the recent movements of one large bandit group, Robin used a regular search engine map to find a year-old satellite view of the Mile End landfill site.

As the city of Locksley had declined, Gisborne Waste Management gradually bought up deserted suburbs, bulldozed buildings, and turned Robin's home town into a money-spinning dump for the rest of the country's waste.

Robin already knew about Gisborne's landfill sites, because his dad used to rant about how scandalous it was and because constructing Gisborne's newest dump involved flattening the house that the Hood family had lived in for four generations.

But as he scrolled around satellite images of Locksley, Robin was still shocked at how much of the city was now being used to dump trash.

Mile End Landfill was in Locksley's northernmost suburbs, and Robin zoomed and scrolled until he identified a giant green mound with the gravel oval at the top. The layout matched the location Alan had described from the night before. Robin went to full zoom and found the stepped path that Nick Adale had walked down.

At the bottom of the path was a building made from a metal cargo container, with several huge grey chimneys rising out of the ground at its rear. Robin could even make out a blurry figure in an orange suit working nearby.

Now that he'd located the site, Robin would be able to get a live satellite feed and higher-resolution pictures using the Super's link to a hacked Chinese spy satellite network, but he had enough information for now.

Next Robin did an internet search for *landfill site accident*. He was surprised to get thousands of results, led by a TV news story showing a housing estate built on top of an old landfill site that had blown up, and a gruesome video showing scavengers running desperately as fire swept across a landfill site in Columbia.

Robin deep-dived into how landfill sites work and why they blow up. He found the website of a Canadian waste disposal corporation with a cute, animated diagram showing how a landfill site was supposed to be built.

The animation showed a kind of giant garbage lasagne. After cartoon diggers made a huge hole and lined it with thick plastic, layers of garbage were dropped down, each level separated by more plastic with lots of drainage pipes running between them.

The Canadian-accented voiceover explained that once a landfill site was capped off, the trash below ground would keep rotting for up to thirty years, gradually releasing a toxic liquid called leachate – and explosive methane gas.

This research, along with what Robin knew about Guy Gisborne's character and the stuff Alan told him about the night before, was enough for him to make a reasonable guess about what had led to the deaths of Heirani and two other workers.

Everyone knew Guy Gisborne was stingy, and Robin felt sure that Mile End Landfill would have been built in the cheapest way possible. When the pipes that were supposed to drain leachate got blocked, Gisborne had recruited a crew of desperate Forest People to crawl through the filth and unblock the pipes.

When they hit a pocket of gas, the resulting explosion killed two workers and left Heirani horribly burned. And rather than take Heirani to hospital, where questions would be asked about how she got injured, Gisborne calculated that it was safer to cover up all evidence of the accident by having her killed . . .

'You nasty, lowlife scumbag,' Robin spat, thumping on the desk in front of him and wondering what to do next.

Locksley police were in Gisborne's pocket, so there was no point calling the cops, and the gangster's thugs had probably done a professional job disposing of bodies and cleaning up the scene of the explosion.

He took out his phone and called Alan, who managed a slight laugh when he answered.

'You show up on my caller display as *Probable Nuisance Call*.'

'Gotta ghost my location,' Robin said. 'And nobody will suspect it's me if they check your call log.'

'Smart,' Alan admitted.

'Are you feeling any better this morning?'

'I feel like I'm living the worst day of my life,' Alan said. 'I got zero sleep. Couldn't stop thinking about Heirani. At breakfast my dad acted all happy, like last night didn't happen – cutting up grapefruit, singing tunes and making fart jokes with my sister. I can't look at him without wanting to puke.'

'I did some research into why landfill sites explode,' Robin said. 'But you can bet Gisborne's people will do a decent job covering up all the evidence.'

'I did a bit of digging myself,' Alan said. 'But I can't go too deep in case my dad looks at my internet search history.'

'Makes sense,' Robin agreed.

'What about Heirani Stone?' Alan asked. 'Did you find out who she was?'

'I'm going to try looking her up,' Robin said. 'But Forest People don't have public records and tend to use false names, so it won't be easy to work out where she came from. There's one other thing we can try, but it's risky for you.'

'What?' Alan asked.

'Gisborne and your dad are bound to have a conversation about what happened over the next few days, right?'

'For sure,' Alan agreed. 'They work side by side every day.'

'I can send you a spyware program,' Robin explained. 'If you can get your hands on your dad's phone and install this spyware app it will send us a copy of every message he sends, record all his phone calls, and even use the microphone to record normal conversations.'

'He uses the iris scanner to unlock his phone, though,' Alan said.

'There's a million ways around that,' Robin said. 'I just need to know what model phone he's using.'

Alan paused and sighed. 'It feels weird going against my own family.'

'Don't do anything that makes you uncomfortable,' Robin urged. 'We can try and keep your dad from getting busted, but who knows what we'll unearth once we start digging.'

After another pause, Alan sounded bitter. 'You know what?' he spat. 'My dad was in charge, but he stood there while they took Heirani away to be murdered. Send me that spyware and damn the consequences. My dad deserves whatever he gets.'

11. THE HOMEWORK FACTORY

Alan had picked up Heirani's card wallet, but all he'd found inside were a few crumpled twenty-pound notes and a stash of little rectangular photos of a teenage Heirani and some friends messing around in a photo booth.

Robin used the Super to search stolen records of driving licences, birth certificates, bank accounts and medical records from more than fifty countries, but found nobody called Heirani Stone in any of them.

His next step would be to run a facial recognition search on Heirani and the other people in the photo booth snaps that Alan had photographed and messaged through. But even with supercomputer power this would take days, and the Super would slow to a crawl while it sought a match amidst the billions of photographs in its data lake.

Since the thugs had described Heirani as *forest scum*, Robin considered asking around and seeing if any of the

Forest People who came to Sherwood Castle's weekly market knew her. But someone might tell Gisborne that Robin was sniffing around, so he decided to park that thought and call Little John instead.

Robin's idea was that his big brother could invite himself to girlfriend Clare's house and use the opportunity to install spyware on Guy Gisborne's home network.

'Not a chance!' John answered touchily. 'I nearly got sent to a super tough military school when I helped you to spy on my mum. There's no way I'm gonna risk wrecking my relationship with Clare by spying on her dad.'

Robin tutted. 'Gisborne murdered *three* people. Don't you care?'

'Of *course* I care,' John said. 'I've helped you before. I'm sure I'll help you again someday. But sometimes you have to look out for number one. I've got exams coming up, I like my school. I just made the senior rugby squad and I've got a great girlfriend. I'm not putting everything that's good in my life in jeopardy every time you cook up some crazy scheme. And maybe you should start thinking like that too.'

Robin scowled at his phone. 'What does that mean?'

John huffed. 'Look what happened to Marion on your watch.'

Robin felt like he'd been stabbed in the gut. He almost yelled, *that's not fair*, but realised it would sound babyish. After a pause, John resumed speaking.

'I'm serious, Robin. You're into this whole justice thing. Take from the rich, give to the poor. Save the world. Take on every bad guy you encounter. But have you noticed that a lot of those rich, powerful people don't like that? Do you ever stop and ask yourself where you're going to end up?'

Robin saw some sense in his brother's words, but his anger swept that aside. 'I'd rather get killed or spend my life in prison than be a coward, living in gold-plated luxury with money stolen by Sheriff Marjorie.'

'You're exactly like our dad,' John snapped back. 'And look where his mighty principles got him.'

'Don't help if you don't want to,' Robin said irritably. 'But spare me the lecture. I'm going. I've got heaps to do.'

'Wait,' John said, as Robin's finger hovered over the *end call* button.

Robin hoped Little John had changed his mind, but he changed the subject.

'There's something else I was going to call you about,' John began. 'I spoke to Dad's lawyer, Tybalt Bull, on Friday. Dad's appeal hearing could be called into court any day now. Tybalt wants to talk to you about it, but the number he has for you didn't work.'

Robin thought for a second. 'I haven't spoken to Tybalt since D'Angela reprogrammed my phone to make it properly untraceable. The software probably blocks his number. Why does he want to talk to me?'

'Tybalt's job is to get Dad out of prison by convincing people that he's a good person who didn't steal computers and beat up two cops,' John explained. 'He wants you to try and stay out of trouble until after Dad's appeal, because having a thirteen-year-old son who's a one-person crime wave doesn't make Dad look so great.'

Robin felt like he got blamed for everything. He sighed deeply. 'Tell Tybalt to call me anytime. I'll add him to my safe contacts list.'

'Gotta go pack my bag to get back to boarding school tomorrow,' John said. 'Try to stay out of prison.'

Robin grunted as his brother hung up. He felt like throwing his phone at the wall or kicking something, but his mood elevated when Josie came up the stairs into the Nest. She held a red plastic tray with giant bacon baps and hot chocolate from one of the food outlets in the castle atrium.

'Well, don't you look cheerful?' Josie said sarcastically.

Robin enjoyed looking at her hair, caught in sunlight coming through the skylights. As Josie put the food down on Robin's desk, he breathed her smell and realised that she was the best thing in his life right now.

'Every time I speak to my brother it does my head in,' Robin complained, then smiled and gave her a kiss. 'I thought you were broke. Where'd you get money for breakfast?'

'Stole twenty from the dirty jeans on your bedroom floor,' Josie admitted unapologetically. 'You've got loads of money.'

Robin laughed as he peeled back foil and bit his warm bap. 'Family all OK last night?' he asked.

Josie shrugged. 'How should I know? My dad insists that I sit in on the family group chat every Saturday, but they all babble away in Albanian or Italian. I can't understand a word.'

'Did you read the message I sent about what my friend Alan witnessed?'

'Sounds horrific,' Josie said, as she blew on her hot chocolate. 'I know you're going to get all obsessed with this dead Heirani girl, but we did agree to do our History projects this morning. I got a final warning for missing my last two homeworks. My dad will flip if I miss another.'

'Two missing homeworks is nothing,' Robin snorted. 'I've missed four, and I can't count how many lessons I've skipped since new year.'

'But you don't share a room with a big hairy father who shouts and threatens to ground you and take your phone away,' Josie said, as she settled in an office chair and thumped her trashed Adidas Superstars on the desktop.

Josie knew getting muddy shoes near the air intakes of Robin's precious supercomputer would irritate him. Robin knew she was doing it to tease, and didn't take the bait.

'And I've sorted homework,' Robin said, as he wheeled his chair backwards and woke up the computer at another desk.

'You wrote your essay?' Josie asked.

'Not exactly,' Robin said, as he opened a text document and signalled for Josie to look at the screen. 'I found this outfit in Vietnam through one of my hacking forums. You send them homework in any subject and they charge five US dollars a page to do it for you. It looks fake if it's too perfect, so I told the guy to write two different essays, one for me that's a B grade, and a C minus for you.'

'C minus!' Josie said crossly, as she read the essay on screen. 'I'm *way* better at History than you.'

Robin laughed as he chewed the last bit of bacon bap. 'I'm kidding, I bought you an A minus. All we have to do is to copy them out in our own handwriting.'

'This is a really good essay,' Josie said, as she read from the screen. 'Saves me a whole Sunday afternoon. But you're sure it's OK? What if teachers find out somehow?'

'This guy has hundreds of five-star reviews,' Robin explained. 'I wound up with a heap of cryptocurrency sticks after we robbed Mindy Burger, and what better way to spend it than getting some guy in Vietnam to do all of our homework for the next five years?'

'Did we beat homework?' Josie beamed, as she stepped up behind Robin's chair and gently kissed his neck. 'You might just be the best boyfriend ever!'

'Well, obviously,' Robin replied.

12. SAUSAGE DOG LIMBO

The Super had so far drawn a blank trying to find information about Heirani Stone, but there were people Robin hoped might help, and he began by video-calling the TV presenter Lynn Hoapili.

She'd broadcast some of the first stories about Robin's rebel activities on local news and after Robin let her interview him for a TV special, she'd been promoted to a prestigious national presenter job on *World at Seven*.

But Lynn only managed a sigh when Robin told her what Alan had witnessed the night before.

'You don't have a story,' she told Robin bluntly. 'You have a friend who claims to have witnessed something. The closest thing to evidence is a card holder with some old photographs of a woman nobody has ever heard of.

'If we broadcast a story claiming that a well-connected man like Guy Gisborne is responsible for the deaths of three people with no solid evidence, he'll sue and I'll get fired.'

'I know it's not the whole story yet,' Robin said pleadingly. 'But doesn't *World at Seven* have experts? Researchers and investigators and stuff? Gisborne's probably gonna be the next Sheriff of Nottingham, so he's not just a local gangster any more.'

Lynn pushed hair off her brow and laughed. 'Do you watch my show, Robin?'

'Not much,' Robin confessed, though *never* would have been the honest answer.

'Yesterday *World at Seven* ran a three-minute segment on a charity limbo race for sausage dogs. We don't have teams of journalists and investigators; we have four low-paid researchers who feel put upon if they have to change the filter in the coffee machine.'

It was another disappointment after Little John had refused to help.

'What if I agreed to do another exclusive interview with you?' Robin asked.

Lynn looked down awkwardly as she replied. 'I don't mean to be rude, Robin, but you're not a red-hot story any more. Last summer you were a big mystery. Who is this crazy pint-sized kid charging around robbing cash machines, flipping cop cars and sticking it to the man? Everyone was painting *Robin Hood Lives* graffiti and wearing *Robin Hood Lives* T-shirts. Now everyone knows who you are.'

Robin sounded cross. 'So, I'm less important than sausage dog limbo?'

'That's why the word *new* is in news,' Lynn explained. 'If you get caught or you do something spectacular, you'll be back in the news.'

'Spectacular, like proving that notorious butt-wipe Guy Gisborne is responsible for the deaths of three people in a gas explosion?'

'One hundred per cent,' Lynn said, laughing slightly. 'I can't help you right now because my boss wants me here in Capital City doing stories on Sheriff Marjorie's presidential campaign. But do you remember Oluchi? She might be keen to help.'

'Your old Channel Fourteen intern,' Robin said.

'Oluchi is trying to make a name for herself as a freelance journalist and videographer, selling articles and video clips to news outlets. She's a good journalist, she works hard, and it would be a huge step up if she broke a story proving that the next Sheriff of Nottingham is a murderer.'

Lynn bounced Oluchi's contact details across and Robin left a message on her phone. By this time, he'd received an email from his hacking mentor D'Angela detailing the best ways for Alan to get spyware on his dad's phone and laptop.

Robin forwarded Alan all the information and a link to download the spyware, then Oluchi called back, sounding keen to help. She agreed to come to Sherwood Castle, provided she could get a safe escort through the forest.

While Robin was a frenzy of activity, Josie sat in front of a screen a couple of metres away, looking bored as she copied her History essay off the screen.

Robin called Jeanne next. She was a French mechanical engineer who lived in Sherwood Castle with her handyman husband Unai. She'd helped Robin stop Sheriff Marjorie destroying huge chunks of Sherwood Forest during the previous summer's floods, and said she'd be happy to join the team and help with technical information about waste disposal sites.

'Now where are you off to?' Josie asked, when Robin sprang for the stairs.

'The Scarlocks' office,' Robin said. 'They hate the idea of Guy Gisborne getting elected sheriff more than anyone, and if I'm going to get this dirtbag I need all the help I can get.'

'And how exactly are you going to *get this dirtbag*?' Josie asked.

'I'm working on it . . .' Robin said weakly.

'Can I come with you?'

'Free country,' Robin answered.

Will Scarlock looked irritated when Robin and Josie charged into his office, but the rebels' leader dropped everything when he heard what Gisborne had done and began setting up a big meeting at two that afternoon.

Besides Robin and Josie, Will invited rebel security chief Azeem, his sons Neo and Sam, plus Jeanne the engineer and her husband Unai. Wannabe journalist

Oluchi was last to arrive, breathless and spattered with mud after being escorted through the forest by a security team on a pair of quad bikes.

Sam Scarlock gave Oluchi a damp flannel to wipe her face as Will started the meeting by reminding them all that Guy Gisborne would make life miserable for everyone in Sherwood Forest if he became sheriff. Will also said they needed to act swiftly, because the chances of finding evidence linking Gisborne to the three dead Forest People shrank with every passing hour.

Lots of ideas got bounced around, but the team reached a consensus that there were three ways to get evidence, and they needed to try all of them.

The first was for Robin to keep hacking, finding ways to get spyware on Guy Gisborne and Nick Adale's equipment, while trying to find information on Heirani Stone and the other two victims.

Azeem agreed that she and a couple of her most trusted security officers would try to find other Forest People who'd worked on Gisborne's landfill sites. But they'd have to be discreet, because they didn't want the gangster finding out that they were on his case.

Lastly, and most controversially, the group decided that it was worth sending a team to look inside the Mile End landfill site. Their task would be to check out the area where the gas explosion took place, take photos and video of any damage, and try to find something Gisborne's thugs had missed when they cleaned up the evidence.

13. ORANGE OVERALLS

Guy Gisborne promised voters that if he became sheriff, he'd crack down on Forest People working illegally and stealing jobs from tax-paying citizens. But in truth, the gangster always hired the cheapest workers he could get. Azeem had no trouble finding Sherwood Castle rebels who'd worked at Mile End Landfill, including one of her own security officers.

An hour after the meeting in Will's office, the rebel team had several well-worn sets of Gisborne Waste Management branded overalls, along with details of staff parking areas, security procedures, and gaps in the fence where workers snuck out for smoke breaks.

Robin was a thrill-seeker and keen to be involved with anything risky, but he accepted that a kid wandering around a landfill site was suspicious. So he spent Sunday afternoon using the Super to find a live satellite feed that covered Mile End Landfill, then he scanned nearby transmissions until he locked on to the radio frequency used by landfill site staff.

This radio traffic was just workers coordinating the stream of trucks tipping rubbish, but Robin thought he might pick up a report if a worker spotted someone suspicious.

The team who put on battered orange overalls would be led by a rebel security officer named Ísbjörg. The petite twenty-two-year-old Icelander had spent her late teens driving one of Mile End's massive bulldozers, so she knew her way around the site.

Jeanne's engineering skills made her the next obvious choice, and the quartet was completed by journalist Oluchi and Will Scarlock's youngest son, Neo.

They arrived at Mile End in a Saab older than some of its passengers. Staff car park number three was near empty on this chilly Sunday night, and keeping intruders out of a massive trash dump wasn't a priority. The entry gate was unmanned and the quartet kept their faces down as they passed a security camera with a blinking red light.

'Testing comms,' Robin said, from his comfy office chair inside the Nest.

Neo tapped his earpiece radio before answering. 'Hear you loud and clear, Robin.'

'The satellite I'm locked on to is looking through a bit of cloud, but I can see the four of you as red and orange blobs on the infrared camera,' Robin explained.

'Wish you were here instead of me,' Neo told Robin. 'My suit smells of BO and the stench of rubbish burns the back of your throat.'

Ísbjörg knew the site layout and led the group briskly up a gravel path towards the top of the capped western mound. At seven on a Sunday night there were no staff working the area, but the group disturbed rats, gulls and the gangs of feral cats that roamed the site.

They'd reached the oval at the top of the mound when a breeze from the active part of the landfill site sent a particularly nasty smell into Neo's face. He stopped walking as he retched a mouthful of puke into the back of his mouth.

'So nasty!' Neo complained, as he coughed and spat.

Oluchi gave him a bottle of water to wash his mouth out, but Ísbjörg found the display comical.

'They employed a lot of pukers back when I worked here,' Ísbjörg said, before giving Neo a thump on the back. 'They'd never show up for their second day.'

'I'm good,' Neo said, though he wasn't.

As they walked on, Jeanne held a combustible gas detector that she'd borrowed from her husband Unai's toolbox.

'I'm getting methane gas readings way up in the danger zone,' Jeanne told the other three. 'That shouldn't happen on a capped landfill site if the pipework is venting gas correctly.'

'Guy Gisborne cutting corners to save money?' Oluchi said, full of mock shock. 'Never!'

'But this is *really* bad,' Jeanne emphasised. 'If gas can seep up to the surface through thick plastic tanking and five metres of clay soil, there must be huge amounts of explosive gas trapped below our feet.'

'Could it blow?' Oluchi asked. 'The whole mound?'

'Maybe,' Jeanne speculated. 'If there was no wind and the gas built up, then it would just need a bolt of lightning, or even a burst of static electricity from these horrible plastic overalls.'

'Very reassuring,' Neo said, eying his overall suspiciously as Ísbjörg stepped into the gravel oval atop the mound.

'Neo, see if they left any evidence up here,' Ísbjörg ordered. 'I'll take Oluchi and Jeanne down to the explosion site.'

Ísbjörg tapped her earpiece to check in with Robin. 'How's our neighbourhood looking?'

'Plenty of things moving around, but nothing big enough to be human,' Robin answered. 'Josie's listening to the radio traffic from the active part of the site and there's nothing suspicious there either.'

Neo pulled a torch out of his pocket and tried to think about anything but the smell as he inspected the gravel for any sign of what had happened to Heirani.

'This is a catastrophe,' Jeanne said, as she stopped on the downhill path and squished the soggy ground beside the path with the toe of her boot.

Oluchi had taken out a little vlogging camera to record. 'What's the problem?' she asked.

Jeanne realised she was being filmed and made her French accent posher. 'Leachate is supposed to filter through the pipes and get pumped up to the top before being taken away. A properly capped landfill site should have no noticeable smell, but it stinks here and the grass is dying because the soil is toxic.'

There was more shock when the trio reached the little grey building, with corrugated metal walls and thick pipes coming out of the ground at the back. The front door looked brand-new, but its frame was soot-stained and the building's roof had buckled like a tin can in the previous day's explosion.

'Make sure you video all this,' Jeanne told Oluchi as she pointed to a shattered pressure gauge sticking out of the ground. Then she walked around the rear and noticed that the building had an unnatural slant, while its concrete foundation was full of cracks.

Jeanne spoke to Oluchi's camera. 'The trash below our feet has sunk by half a metre since this building was placed here. If the waste pile moves, the pipes that are supposed to drain gas and leachate can get twisted and crushed. That would explain the smell and the gas leaking up through the soil cap.'

'Can that be fixed?' Oluchi asked, holding the camera on Jeanne.

Jeanne scoffed. 'Not by sending a few Forest People down to try unblocking the pipes. To make this landfill properly safe, you'll have to bore down into the trash, install new pipework and some powerful pumps. But that would cost millions.'

As Jeanne spoke, Ísbjörg opened the newly installed door around the front of the building and shone her torch inside.

The metal building's single room contained valves to open and close different pipes, though the computer that controlled them was in bits and its screen melted. Several valves were cracked, and leachate puddled the floor.

Ísbjörg also detected a chlorine smell, like a swimming pool but strong enough to overpower the surrounding atmosphere of rotting trash. Every dry surface was coated in a crusty yellowish skin, and Ísbjörg guessed that Gisborne's thugs had tried to destroy DNA evidence by spraying every surface with bleach.

The thought that two people had died here less than twenty-four hours earlier made Ísbjörg shudder. Then she heard Robin's voice in her earpiece.

'Bad news,' Robin announced. 'I'm picking up a heat signature coming uphill from the main road. Looks like a small car, or a quad bike.'

'How soon?' Ísbjörg asked.

'Very,' Robin answered. 'It'll reach the clearing up top in one minute.'

14. EMPLOYEE OF THE MONTH

'I've found nothing up here,' Neo told his earpiece radio, as he glanced behind and saw headlamps coming through the dark towards the clearing.

'Meet us down here,' Ísbjörg ordered. 'We'll abandon that old Saab and go out the back way.'

Neo ran down the stepped path as fast as darkness and the slippery gravel allowed. He could hear the quad bike on the clearing up top as the grey building came into view. Then a powerful torch beam lit up the ground, forcing Neo to dive off the path before it caught him.

He realised that reflective orange overalls were exactly what he didn't want to be wearing as he crawled across squelchy grass. He found a hiding spot behind a clump of skeletal bushes that were supposed to beautify the mound but had rotted in the toxic soil.

'The important thing is not to be seen,' Ísbjörg reminded everyone over the radio. 'We can't let Gisborne know we're investigating.'

'I can't see anyone else on the satellite images,' Robin added, from the comfort of Sherwood Castle.

Neo tried to ignore the vile-smelling toxic clay that was now smeared across his overall. The torch beam swung back and forth several times, then its owner switched it off and began a slow walk down the path.

'She's speaking into her walkie-talkie,' Neo whispered to his earpiece radio, as he peeked over the bush and saw an obese guard. Her orange suit had *SITE SECURITY* written inside a blue panel on the back.

'Security staff must use a different radio frequency,' Robin answered. 'Josie can't hear what she's saying.'

'The guard looks bored and pissed off,' Neo told everyone. 'She definitely hasn't spotted me.'

He shuffled around the dead bushes to keep out of sight as the security officer passed close by. She kept plodding until she stopped on a flat section of the path and shone her torch down towards the grey building.

Jeanne, Oluchi and Ísbjörg were all out of sight, and the guard was now close enough for Neo to hear what she said to her radio.

'Prakash, do you *really* want me to go all the way down there?' she moaned. 'It's two hundred steps back to the top. My inhaler ran out and these alerts always turn out to be a bird or cat tripping the sensor.'

Neo couldn't hear the crackly response, but it made the guard furious.

'Don't do me any favours, will you, mate?' the guard stormed into her radio. 'Next time I'm behind the security desk and you're out in the cold, I'll make you run a blasted marathon.'

Neo forgot the stench for long enough to smirk as he spoke quietly to the others on his radio. 'They say you get what you pay for, and I suspect Gisborne's security people are very badly paid. The guard is coming your way, but she won't be hard to dodge.'

Ísbjörg replied. 'Gisborne's guys did a good job destroying any forensic evidence down here, but there are clear signs of a recent explosion and Oluchi has got some interesting video. Now we're going to circle around over the grass to the opposite side of the mound. Can you cut across and meet us?'

'Should be fine,' Neo said. 'Robin, is there any sign of more guards?'

'No heat signatures within half a kilometre,' he answered.

Neo needed the guard to clear off before he could escape, but she stood still, catching her breath, then pulled a pack of cigarettes from her jacket pocket. He remembered Jeanne's gas detector readings and half expected the woman to go up in flames, but there was a breeze whipping across the mound. She took one long drag on the cigarette before sauntering on down towards the grey building.

After crossing the gravel path, Neo found his boots lifting up chunks of soggy turf that had failed to grow roots into the toxic clay beneath. He lost concentration when he spotted Ísbjörg leading the others uphill, and his boot sploshed into a deep mudhole and got stuck.

Neo thought he might have to pull his foot out of the boot to move on, but after three attempts there was a big squelchy fart sound. His boot was free, but he was grossed out by the icy leachate soaking his sock.

As Neo stood back up, he realised that the hole he'd stepped into looked weird. It was a three-metre-long trench, running in a straight line. The line pointed directly towards the grey building, as if a projectile had landed at speed after the explosion.

The moonlight wasn't great and Neo couldn't use his torch with the security guard nearby. After a lot of squinting and fumbling, his eye caught a piece of reflective material sticking above the waterline at the far end of the flooded hole.

Neo excitedly tapped his earpiece radio. 'Guys, I might have something.'

He stepped lightly to avoid getting his boot stuck again. When he reached down and grabbed the reflective material, icy brown water squelched out and he realised he was grasping a padded foam strap.

'What is it?' Ísbjörg asked.

'A backpack, I think.'

Neo's boot slipped as he pulled the strap hard. There was a monster sucking sound and mud splattered Neo's trousers as he lifted the pack out. His best guess was that someone had left their pack outside the building before starting work. When the explosion blew the door off, the backpack had been scorched and thrown fifty metres uphill.

'Have you got it?' Oluchi asked.

'What's inside?' Robin added. 'Are you sure it's not random trash?'

Once the worst of the mud and liquid had dropped off, Neo tried to open the pack.

'The plastic zip has melted shut,' Neo told everyone as he tugged. 'What could have caused that except heat from an explosion?'

The zip was wrecked, but eventually Neo pulled hard enough to break the stitching holding it in place.

'Here we go!' Neo said triumphantly as he peered into the backpack and saw puddled brown water, partially covering door keys, a sandwich wrapped in cling film, two tangerines, some bits of paper, an *I love Las Vegas* bobble hat and a smartphone.

'That security guard is still around,' Ísbjörg warned, as she saw Neo striding out of the dark towards her. 'Let's clear out and study what you've found later.'

15. MONDAY MORNING BLUES

Alan used to be proud of his bedroom. One entire wall was devoted to shelves for his collection of boxed limited-edition trainers. He had a gaming PC that lit up like a Christmas tree, a drone, and expensive clothes that he'd grow out of before he ever got to wear them.

But now all this stuff seemed like bribes from two workaholic parents who'd sooner give him their credit card details than their time.

'You look like crap,' eleven-year-old Dakota observed, as Alan wandered into the kitchen. He was usually super neat, but he had wild hair, toothpaste down his shirt, and wore the baggy shorts he'd slept in.

'Restless night,' Alan moaned, as he scratched the back of his leg.

The spacious kitchen was the heart of the house, with quartz worktops and fancy German appliances. But his dad didn't cook and their cleaner had quit, so they lived off takeout and there was mess everywhere.

'You'll never make the school bus,' Dakota told her brother as he looked in the cupboard and saw that the only cereal was one that he hated.

'You're not Mum,' Alan said irritably. 'Who even cares if I'm late for school?'

Alan glowered at his sister as he gulped orange juice out of the carton. Dakota wore purple Locksley High team socks tucked into black leggings and her school pack had rugby boots and an energy drink wedged into the mesh pockets on the outside.

Alan had made zero new friends since Robin ran away. He envied his sister's sporty social group, along with her ability to sleep at night, because she hadn't witnessed a horribly burned woman getting dragged off and shoved in the boot of a car.

'You're just a Monday morning cliché,' Dakota said wearily, as she slid off her stool at the breakfast counter. She gave her big brother the finger before grabbing her overstuffed pack. 'I'm outta here.'

Alan felt miserable, and dreaded the prospect of a day in school. He'd barely slept, there were no cool people in his class, his sister was a pain, his mum was barely part of his life any more and his dad was a cold-blooded killer.

He threw the empty juice carton at the overflowing kitchen bin and slammed the fridge door angrily. It was lucky Dakota was gone, because she'd have laughed her arse off when the door bounced and hit him in the face.

As Alan rubbed his nose, flung a cereal box and unleashed a string of foul swear words, he spotted his dad's keys and laptop on the dining table.

Alan had tried getting hold of his dad's phone or laptop since Robin sent instructions for installing spyware the day before. This was the first time he'd seen either device out of his dad's hands, but it wasn't the opportunity he needed. He could hear his dad moving around upstairs and he'd soon be down to pick up his stuff and drive to work.

Since Alan could no longer stand being in the same room as his dad, he decided to go back to his room and hide until after he left. It meant he'd be even later for school, but Monday's first lesson was Geography, and if he was going to get in trouble for being late, he figured that he might as well be super late and miss a whole boring lesson.

Unfortunately, Alan crossed his dad on the stairs. Even worse, Nick Adale was keeping up his cheerful *let's pretend you never saw me let some poor girl get murdered* act.

'I heard Dakota go out,' Nick Adale said, as Alan backed up to the stair rail to let him by. 'Shouldn't you be gone too?'

'Woke up late,' Alan answered. 'I'll get the city bus.'

'Up late on X-Box again?' Nick asked breezily, as he reached the bottom of the stairs and pushed his feet into a pair of tan brogues. 'I didn't get round to booking the supermarket delivery, so how about Wally's Steakhouse tonight? I shouldn't be home late and Dakota said she's happy to eat lobster.'

'Sure,' Alan said, though the prospect of dinner with Dakota's snarkiness, Dad's jokes and Gisborne's thuggish cronies dropping by the table to tell him that he'd grown was about as appealing as having a tooth pulled.

'I'd drop you at school but I'm going in the other direction,' Nick said.

'City bus is fine,' Alan said, as he stepped into the bathroom he shared with Dakota.

He flipped the window open because his sister had gone nuts with her body spray. Then he turned on the shower, hoping the hot blast would wake him up and make him feel less anxious and angry.

After showering, Alan decided he was going to take his sweet time, dry his hair with a hairdryer and fix his afro properly instead of tying his hair back.

The only towel on the rail was wet and smeared in Dakota's moisturiser. As he reached into the cupboard under the sink to take a clean one, the bathroom door crashed open so hard that the top hinge ripped out of the frame.

'What the—' Alan gasped, jumping with fright as a huge man loomed in the doorway.

He wore a grimy black tracksuit and had *Killer* tattooed on his vast neck. After giving Alan a slap that sent him sprawling sideways over the toilet bowl, the giant grabbed one of Alan's skinny ankles, then yanked him across the slippery bathroom floor and out into the hallway.

'Do you know who my dad is?' Alan spat, as his naked body slammed into the hallway wall.

'Your dad is Nick Adale,' the man growled as he stepped back into the bathroom and threw Alan his shorts. 'My name is Killer, and you are a dirty little grass who's been talking to his friends in the forest.'

Alan hurt all down his left side as he pulled the shorts over his feet. Downstairs there were several scary guys with deep voices and his dad was yelling furiously at them.

'You get Guy Gisborne on the phone,' Nick demanded. 'We've worked together for two decades. This *has* to be a misunderstanding.'

'Gisborne sent us here with specific instructions,' one deep voice boomed. 'So shut the smart mouth and put your hands back on top of your head. Unless you fancy another slap.'

Alan thought he'd been careful. He had no idea how they knew he'd been in touch with Robin. But his most immediate problem was that his legs were wet from the shower and the shorts stuck to his skin as he tried to pull them up.

'Stop messing about!' Killer roared.

'Can't help it!' Alan protested, as Killer grabbed his ankle again.

'Waste my time,' Killer growled, 'Then go downstairs the hard way.'

'No,' Alan begged as Killer walked backwards, dragging Alan by the ankle, his shorts stuck halfway up his legs.

This time it was over carpet. Alan howled in pain as the friction rubbed skin off his bare arse. As Alan was about to get painfully dragged down sixteen stairs, Killer misjudged his backwards walk and stumbled over the top step.

As the huge man grasped the stair rail to save himself, he let Alan go. The teenager crawled forward then scrambled to his feet. His bum and thigh were rubbed raw, but he managed to tug his shorts up and sprint down the hallway towards his bedroom.

Killer let out a massive roar. 'You do not want to mess with me.'

Alan was terrified as he ran into his room. He snatched his phone off its charging plate and put on a pair of Crocs. Then he scrambled around the end of his bed and opened his first-floor window.

He'd seen Robin jump from this height, but had never been brave enough to try it himself. Alan hesitated, with one foot on the window ledge, but found all the courage he needed when Killer blasted through his bedroom door and made a lunge for him.

'I'll stick your head through the wall!' Killer shouted as Alan flew through fresh morning air.

He landed hard, jarring his ankle and losing one Croc as his phone spun across the drive towards his dad's big Mercedes.

Killer shook his enormous fist out of the first-floor window and shouted to some colleagues standing by a pickup, 'Don't let the brat get away.'

Alan glanced backwards as he found his feet and saw a pair of Gisborne's thugs lumbering towards him. The carpet burn on his arse was bleeding and his body hurt in ten places, but he had to run.

16. SCHOOL ZONE

Josie joined Robin and the unruly Maid family for Monday breakfast. Then the pair grabbed their school packs and headed down to the row of first-floor conference rooms that the rebels had converted into classrooms.

School Zone now served two hundred kids who lived inside Sherwood Castle, and eighty who came in from the forest each morning. Things were always chaotic, with pupils aged between five and eighteen, many of whom didn't speak English as their first language. There was also a lack of supplies and all teachers were unpaid volunteers.

'If I can keep my head down . . .' Robin told Josie hopefully as he came off the stairs into a carpeted hallway filled with noisy kids waiting to be let into morning registration.

'Don't bet on it,' Josie said. 'Principal Khan has it in for you. But at least you did your History project.'

Robin shook his head. 'I paid to get the essay written, but I was busy last night, so I still haven't copied it out in my own handwriting.'

'So how many is that?' Josie asked, smirking and shaking her head. 'Six homeworks in a row you've missed?'

Robin didn't answer because they'd reached four kids their own age, who they did most of their lessons with. A bulky forest boy called Lucius thumped Robin on the back. 'Happy Monday – what have you lovebirds been up to?'

'Not much,' Robin said, as he caught Lucius' pungent aroma of sweat and forest dirt.

It wasn't the forest kids' fault that they smelled bad, but that didn't stop them from smelling bad. And all the forest kids claimed Sherwood Castle kids had gone soft since they got electricity and they started taking regular showers.

'Get this,' Josie explained to the others. 'Robin *thinks* he can stay out of trouble if he keeps his head down, but I'm prepared to bet my whole week's lunch money that he'll get dragged into Mr Khan's office before morning break.'

Lucius nodded in agreement, then looked at Robin. 'You might be OK if you've done your History project.'

The hallway was getting noisier as more kids rocked up for school. Three little kids charged through the gap between them, one catching Robin with her lunchbox.

Josie beamed. 'Well, Robin has *almost* done his History project . . .'

'Shut up.' Robin groaned.

Lucius and red-headed twins called Sarah and Jennifer all burst out laughing.

'We should bet how much detention Robin gets,' Lucius said cheerfully. 'I say five hours minimum.'

The bell for morning registration saved Robin from more teasing, but not from the wrath of Khan. As Josie and thirty other kids aged between eleven and fourteen filed into classroom number four, Robin felt the school principal's hand on his shoulder.

'Mr Hood, a word!' Khan said cockily.

Josie and several other classmates poked out tongues or cheerfully sang *you're in trouble*. Robin groaned as the lanky ex-police officer led him to a cluttered office that looked exactly like every other school office Robin had ever stood in.

'You're not stupid,' Mr Khan began, as he sat in the chair behind his desk. 'You know why you're here.'

Robin slumped in the chair opposite, which made Khan thump his desk.

'Did I say you could sit down?' Khan barked.

Robin tutted and muttered, 'It's not the army, you know?' as he stood up again.

'Since new year, I've had several complaints about you messing around in class. You've missed six days of school and handed in less than *half* of your homework.

'It's almost as if you don't take school seriously. Almost as if you feel that the famous Robin Hood doesn't have to follow school rules. Well, let me tell you, Robin, every pupil who enters School Zone is the same, whether you're in an online video with a hundred million views, or you're a six-year-old flood victim who's too shy to speak his name.'

Robin's mischievous side was tempted to say *actually, it's three hundred million views* and see if that made Mr Khan's head explode. But he was also smart enough to know that this meeting and his punishment would go faster if he nodded politely and kept his trap shut.

'A lot of kids, especially the younger boys, look to you as a role model,' Mr Khan continued. 'But the example you're currently setting is shockingly—'

Khan stopped speaking abruptly as Robin's phone started playing 'Papa's Got a Brand New Pigbag' by Pigbag.

'Phones should be switched off during school hours,' Mr Khan said, eyes bulging as he stood up from his desk. 'Give me the handset, *now!*'

Robin took out his ringing phone. He planned to hand it over until he saw that the message came from the encrypted gaming server he was using to contact Alan Adale.

'I *have* to take this,' Robin said awkwardly.

'You certainly will not!' Mr Khan roared. 'Hand me the phone. Don't you *dare* answer.'

'Alan,' Robin said, as he answered.

'Gisborne's guys showed up and dragged me out of the shower,' Alan blurted desperately. 'They seem to know everything.'

'Seriously?' Robin gasped, backing away from Mr Khan as the teacher tried to snatch the phone. 'Where are you now?'

'I demand that phone *now*!' Mr Khan shouted, marching furiously around to Robin's side of the desk.

'I tried to run but they cornered me,' Alan said. 'I doubled back, and now I'm up a tree in my neighbours' garden. The thugs are too fat to climb, but they've got me surrounded.'

'I'll do everything I can,' Robin said, as Mr Khan grabbed his arm.

'I'm scared they're going to kill me, like Heirani,' Alan said.

Robin didn't hear what Alan said next because his phone clattered to the office floor.

'This is serious,' Robin shouted to Mr Khan as he tried to pick up the phone. 'My friend is in danger.'

'Nothing is more serious than your education!' Mr Khan boomed back, eyes bulging and cheeks going red. 'How dare you answer a phone call in my office?'

Robin picked the phone off the carpet and tried to scramble out of the room.

'Hang on one second, Alan,' he said.

Mr Khan blocked his office door. Robin glanced over his shoulder at the clutter on Khan's desk and picked up a big metal hole punch.

'If you'd just listen and stop being a stubborn idiot,' Robin told Khan, then strained as he threw the hole punch as hard as he could.

Khan raised a hand, but he was too slow and the hole punch whacked him full in the face. As Mr Khan stumbled sideways, Robin charged and got the door open enough to slither into the hallway.

Robin's stomach was turning somersaults and he was horrified by what he'd done to a teacher. Then he remembered why he'd done it and put his phone up to his face.

'Alan, you still there? Alan?' Robin repeated, but the call was dead.

Gisborne's thugs will kill him.

Probably torture him for information first.

How can I help him?

'Robin Hood, don't bother coming back here,' Mr Khan steamed as he stumbled out of his office with one hand over his injured face. 'You are expelled from School Zone.'

Robin didn't look back as he sprinted past a couple of late-arriving forest kids then hurtled down a set of fire stairs, heading for the Nest.

17. FLYING GNOME

It would have looked comical from a distance: Alan Adale stuck up a tree in his neighbour's back yard, dressed only in a pair of shorts. Two beefy men barked at Alan to get down, while a third picked a garden gnome off the patio and chucked it at him.

The gnome clattered harmlessly through the branches, but Killer had found a bright yellow stun gun in the back of his car and was marching over.

'What on earth is going on?' a posh woman shouted as she slid her patio door open.

'Mind your business, you old bat,' Killer shouted, then held up the bright yellow taser so that Alan got a good view. 'Climb down now, or I bring you down with fifty thousand volts.'

'That's the deluxe model,' another thug added with a smirk. 'So, it's eighty thousand.'

Alan knew it was hopeless, and started coming down. As soon as he was within reach, one thug grabbed his foot. His bare back scraped branches as he got pulled down, then the guy threw Alan over his shoulder and marched him back home.

Nick Adale still knelt on the kitchen floor with his hands behind his head. Alan got dropped hard onto the floor tiles and received a boot in the gut that sent him writhing back against the kitchen island.

'Not so clever now, are you?' Killer laughed.

'I'm sure this is all a mistake,' Nick Adale said desperately.

A thug in the background ripped a door off a kitchen cabinet, while another smashed a wall mirror with his elbow.

'If I can speak to Guy Gisborne, I'm sure we can clear this up.'

'Don't worry, Nicky boy, you've got a lunch date with Gisborne,' Killer told him. 'You can explain why your son has been grassing us up to Robin Hood. And if I was you, I'd try to think of some good reasons why the boss shouldn't take you down to his basement and use his whips on you.'

Nick glanced sideways at his son, who'd managed to prop his back against the kitchen island.

'It's not true, Dad,' Alan said pleadingly. 'They can check my email; they can check my phone and everything.'

'You and Robin did a good job hiding your calls,' Killer told Alan, as he pointed up at a smoke alarm on the ceiling. 'But Mr Gisborne didn't get to his elevated position by blindly trusting his top people. When your dad got his big promotion, he had every room in this house bugged.'

Alan gulped.

'Tell the truth,' Nick Adale hissed at his son. 'Did you speak to Robin yesterday?'

'Dad, I'm sorry,' Alan said, fighting back tears.

There was a big crash as one of Gisborne's thugs wrecked something in another room.

'I warned you a hundred times to tell me if Robin ever got in touch,' Nick spat furiously. 'You know the kind of person I work for. This isn't a game, you know?'

'I know it's not a game,' Alan yelled back. 'Like it wasn't for Heirani.'

'Who?' Nick asked.

Alan realised his dad had never heard her name. 'The woman who got shoved in the trunk of that Honda,' he shouted.

Killer interrupted by grasping a giant pepper grinder and smashing it to bits against the kitchen counter right above Alan's head.

'As fascinating as this family banter is, I have a busy morning of beatings and debt collections to be getting along with,' Killer said cheerfully. 'Mr Gisborne gave me clear instructions. And he must have a soft spot for young Alan, because you've only been banished.'

'What's that?' Alan asked nervously.

'Banished means *get the hell out of town*,' Killer explained, before looking across at Nick. 'There's a 10:24 train out of Locksley Parkway, heading towards Capital City. Make sure your boy is on that train. If he's seen within a hundred kilometres of Locksley after that, his next ride will be a one-way trip to the bottom of a landfill site.

'After you drop the kid off, you're gonna drive to Wally's Steakhouse. You have a one o'clock lunch reservation with Guy Gisborne. And I'll have one of my colleagues waiting outside Locksley High, so don't try any funny business or—'

Killer's speech was drowned out as one of his goons charged in wielding a golf club and began manically knocking dents in a stainless-steel cooker hood.

'Dave, can you not see I'm speaking here?' Killer shouted.

'Right, boss!' Dave answered, then backed out sheepishly.

Killer looked back at Nick and made a gun with his fingers. 'Like I was saying, sport, show up for that lunch meeting with Mr Gisborne. Otherwise, it'll be my guy who collects Dakota from school.'

18. CHARGING POINT

Oluchi was in the Nest doing more background research when Robin shot up the stairs at five hundred kilometres an hour.

'No school this morning?' she asked.

'It's complicated,' Robin spluttered. 'The education system is built to turn out mindless robots, and I'm not a mindless robot.'

Oluchi looked baffled as Robin crashed into an office chair and switched on his workstation. Robin began telling Oluchi about Alan's desperate call as he downloaded a map showing where Alan lived.

'It's twenty kilometres from here as the crow flies,' Robin calculated. 'Even if I grabbed my bow and a quad bike right now, it would be over before I got there.'

'And you'd be crossing the forest alone, which isn't safe with so many bandits around.'

Robin glanced anxiously at his phone, though he knew it would have pinged if Alan had tried to call back.

'Is there anyone nearer to Alan's house who might help?' Oluchi suggested.

Robin thought for a couple of seconds. 'There are people in Locksley, like Lucy Maid. But they're not equipped to take on Gisborne's thugs with zero notice.'

'I guess we can only wait and hope Alan calls back,' Oluchi said.

Robin pounded furiously on the desktop. 'I *must* have done something wrong. But I only contacted Alan through the game server, which is encrypted and basically undetectable . . .'

'Do you want me to make a hot chocolate?' Oluchi asked. 'It might help you to calm down.'

Robin ignored the offer and moaned desperately. 'Alan's my oldest friend and now Gisborne's gonna do him in. Probably because of some stupid security mistake I made . . .'

Oluchi put a firm hand on Robin's shoulder. 'Alan escaped once; he might do so again. Also, Nick Adale is Gisborne's number two, and you told me that Alan's mum is head of Capital City Metro.'

'What's that got to do with anything?' Robin asked.

'Gisborne can easily wipe out Forest People who nobody will come looking for. But he's trying to get elected as Sheriff of Nottingham, and lots of awkward questions will get asked if a senior employee and his son vanish in the middle of an election campaign.'

Robin hadn't considered this, and felt relieved. 'Alan reckons his mum has abandoned him and Dakota, but I guess she's important enough for Gisborne to be worried. Like, she's been to receptions at the Presidential Palace and she gets on TV news when the train drivers go on strike.'

'So, all is not lost,' Oluchi said. 'But there's nothing we can do right now.'

'Sitting around waiting is the worst,' Robin complained.

Oluchi stepped across to the workstation she'd been using and picked up a wrinkled paper ticket covered with brown smudges.

'This might keep you occupied,' Oluchi said. 'And take your mind off things.'

'What is it?'

'I've spoken to a couple of contacts inside the big news organisations,' Oluchi explained. 'They all say the same thing: a story about gas leaking out of a poorly constructed landfill site isn't big news. A story about Gisborne covering up an explosion that killed two people is newsworthy, but only if we can find out who the victims were.'

'Was this ticket in the backpack that Neo found?'

Oluchi nodded. 'There were wrappers and receipts scrunched up at the bottom of the backpack. Most had turned to mush, but this one looks like a charging receipt for an electric vehicle. It's got the logo of the company that runs the charging station, a customer number, charging times and last Thursday's date. There's no customer name or vehicle registration number, but perhaps someone with your skills can hack the account and find out who that customer is?'

This was the kind of challenge Robin loved and he thought for a few seconds before answering. 'I can start by checking my hacking forums to see if there have been any data breaches at the charging company. Maybe we can get an account password or some other information off the phone we found in the bag.'

'I checked the phone when I got here this morning,' Oluchi said. 'You can still see muddy water trapped behind the screen when you shake it.'

Robin nodded. 'There's a lady in the market who fixes phones. We'll have to get her to take it apart and dry everything out properly. If I try to unlock the phone while there's water inside, the battery could short and fry the whole thing.'

'I'm going to ask around and see if we can track the phone repair lady down before market day,' Oluchi said.

Robin checked his own phone for the tenth time, making sure he had a signal and that the ringer volume was at full blast so that he wouldn't miss Alan trying to contact him. Then he looked at the blurry charging receipt.

He started his investigation by finding the charging company's website. Next, he clicked on a map of all their charging stations and realised the only one near the Mile End landfill site was in a service station car park next to Route 24.

'Maybe I can find a CCTV camera on that site,' Robin said, mostly to himself.

He was using an online map to get street view images of the charging station when two adults began stomping up the stairs.

'Thought I'd find you hiding up here,' Will Scarlock snapped furiously.

Robin made an involuntary shudder as Karma reached the top of the stairs and glowered at him.

'Like I don't have enough to deal with!' Karma yelled. 'Attacking your school principal with a hole punch? Did you lose your tiny mind?'

'You did *what*?' Oluchi said, shocked.

'Every staff member in School Zone is a volunteer,' Will ranted. 'They work hard with limited resources for no money, and this is how you treat them?'

'I had to take that call,' Robin said. 'It was Alan Adale. He's in danger.'

'If you were expecting an important call, you should have left your phone with an adult,' Karma said.

'I suppose I could have.' Robin squirmed as the two grown-ups loomed over his workstation. 'I just didn't think about every single detail.'

'You can't run a school where kids get to pick and choose what rules they follow,' Will said.

'Maybe I shouldn't have had my phone,' Robin admitted. 'But Mr Khan was still being pig-headed. He should have let me take the call when I said it was urgent and punished me after. And besides, I didn't throw the hole punch that hard.'

'Really?' Will quizzed. 'So why is Mr Khan in the medical unit? He's waiting for the duty nurse to put stitches in a cut over his eye.'

Robin bit his bottom lip and looked down at his trainers.

'What will you do all day if Mr Khan doesn't let you back into School Zone?' Karma asked. 'You need education. You need qualifications.'

Robin folded his arms and went on the defensive. 'I learn more here in the Nest with the hacking stuff D'Angela sends me than I ever do in class. And what are qualifications going to do for me? If I left the forest, I'd have to serve a million years in prison before I could apply to university or get a straight job.'

'That's the world we live in now,' Will said. 'Things could change for the better in a few years' time.'

'What, when President Marjorie is running the country?' Robin scoffed. 'And I'm sorry I hurt Mr Khan, OK? But he never listens and I couldn't ignore the call when my oldest friend needed help.'

Will sighed and took a step back to reduce the tension. 'We're all going to have to sit around a table and have a *serious* discussion about your behaviour and your future education.'

'And your punishment,' Karma interrupted. 'Matt and the other lads in School Zone look up to Robin and copy everything he does. You can't assault the school principal and get off lightly.'

'To be discussed,' Will said, apparently irritated by Karma's harsh tone. 'But right now, it does seem like your friend Alan needs help. Can you carefully explain where Alan is and what's been happening? Then maybe we can think up a way to help him.'

19. I HOPE YOU'RE PROUD OF YOURSELF

Gisborne's thugs went on a rampage before they left Alan's house, ripping TVs off the walls, lobbing the toaster through a window, shattering the downstairs toilet with a hammer, flushing Dakota's goldfish, setting off two fire extinguishers and stealing Nick Adale's collection of luxury watches.

The clock beside Alan's bed said 09:56. Mercifully the thugs hadn't gone in his room, but he felt sick with nerves and his hands trembled as he stuffed a wheeled case with clothes and sneakers.

'Out of the door in five if you're gonna make that train!' his dad shouted up the stairs.

Alan packed his phone charger, scooped toiletries from the bathroom and found the cash that his nan had sent for his birthday. Then he unlocked his phone and tried to call his mum for the third time, but he kept getting her voicemail.

After dragging his case and a backpack downstairs, Alan crunched over shards of broken mirror in the hallway. His dad, Nick, was in the kitchen, slugging whisky out of a Pyrex jug because all the regular glassware was broken.

'You've got to drive,' Alan reminded his dad. 'I've called Mum a few times but I can't get through to tell her I'm coming.'

Nick poured another huge whisky and blurted, 'I need this booze to calm my nerves.' Then as he walked towards the hallway. 'I guess you'll be happy when they find me in a layby with a bullet through my skull.'

'If Gisborne was going to kill us, wouldn't he have done it already?' Alan asked.

'Gisborne's a sadist who likes to toy with people before he crushes them,' Nick said. 'And he has to be on his best behaviour while he's running for sheriff.'

'I guess I'll keep calling Mum while I'm on the train,' Alan said, feeling a weird cocktail of pity, loathing and love for his dad.

Nick snorted as he brushed past Alan's case and stepped up to a coat rack. 'You're full of bright ideas, so I'm sure you'll figure something out before you get to Capital City.'

As Nick dug his car keys from the pocket of a trench coat, Alan noticed his dad's laptop on the floor in front of the kitchen island.

After a quick glance into the hallway, where his dad stared longingly at a studio portrait of a family that no longer existed, Alan made the split-second decision to take the laptop and drop it down the front pocket of his wheelie case. With luck, his dad would assume it had got smashed or stolen by the thugs.

'Get a move on,' Nick said, slurring and stumbling as he opened the front door.

Alan noticed a cop car parked across the street as he wheeled his case out onto the drive. A neighbour probably called when she heard the house getting trashed, but the officer did nothing once she realised Gisborne's thugs were involved. Nor did she stop Nick getting in the driver's seat of his big Mercedes, though he was obviously drunk.

Alan slid his case across the back seat and sat next to it, because there'd be less awkward eye contact than being next to his dad up front. Nick drove off fast and scraped the front wheel along a kerb. He looked weak and angry as he sped towards Parkway station on the edge of town, while Alan tried to call his mum for the fourth time.

'Try your mother's office,' Nick said. 'Her personal assistant will know where to find her.'

'Good idea,' Alan answered. 'But I don't have her office number.'

Alan felt scared as his drunk dad used one hand to steer and the other to find a number stored on his phone. By the time Nick had texted the number to his son, they'd reached the giant, near-deserted car park of Locksley Parkway station.

'Last time having to chauffeur you around, at least,' Nick slurred resentfully as he parked in a NO STOPPING zone in front of the station's corrugated metal ticket hall. 'Time for my son and his brilliant brain to clear off.'

The 10:24 train could be heard rumbling towards the station as Alan dragged his case off the back seat.

Saying goodbye to his dad felt huge. Alan wanted to ignore the sarcastic comments and say something like *I really hope we can get past this* or *I hope your meeting with Gisborne goes OK.*

Tears welled as he wondered if he'd ever see his dad again. But the train was close and Alan just said, 'Drive careful, you've had a lot to drink,' before shutting the car door.

Nick showed his contempt for his son by lighting up the Mercedes' back tyres and fishtailing across the empty car park. Alan wheeled his heavy case past a broken ticket machine, jogged up a flight of stairs and ran over a bridge to catch the train slowing into the far side platform.

The only other soul on the platform was a skinhead student. She had a portable poster tube filled with artwork. For a paranoid moment Alan imagined there was a gun in the tube and that Gisborne had sent her to assassinate him. But two minutes later he was sitting by the filthy window in an empty train carriage, dialling the number for his mum's assistant.

'Have to talk to my mum as soon as possible,' Alan told the assistant, as the graffiti-strewn outskirts of Locksley moved by at increasing speed.

The assistant spoke like he was reading from a script. 'Mrs Adale will be unable to take calls while she attends the International Public Transit Conference in Berlin. I might be able to schedule a five-minute slot when she returns to her office on Thursday.'

'I'm her *son*,' Alan said firmly. 'I need to speak to my mother *now*.'

'May I suggest that you discuss any issue with your father?' the assistant asked. 'Mrs Adale has made it clear that issues relating to yourself and Dakota should be dealt with by Nick Adale.'

'I need my mum,' Alan said, then groaned. 'Why is that so hard for you to understand?'

'Mrs Adale is currently in a closed ITPC conference session. The best I can do is send her an email flagged as urgent with your contact details. But your mother's diary is *very* full. She doesn't usually return calls unless there is a pre-booked appointment.'

'This is nuts,' Alan said, as he imagined himself rocking up in Capital City in three hours' time with sixty pounds and nowhere to go.

The assistant cleared his throat and sounded cross. 'As I *just* said, Mrs Adale is attending a conference in Berlin. The best I can do send her an email flagged urg—'

'Hello?' Alan said, then moved the phone away from his face and saw that the call had dropped out.

He thought about calling back, but the train had entered a tunnel so there was no point. As Alan stared out the window at brickwork caked in diesel soot, he imagined two possible scenarios.

The best case was that he got to Capital City and lived with his mum and her new bloke, where he clearly wasn't wanted. The worst was that his mum never returned his call and he wound up wandering the streets.

As the train emerged from the tunnel, Alan opened his web browser and typed the IP address of a gaming server from memory. Then he linked to the chat function and poked his oldest friend.

'Alan, thank God!' Robin said when they connected. 'I've been bricking myself since your last call.'

Alan managed a slight laugh. 'Think you were scared? You should see the back of my underwear.'

20. A MILLION THINGS AT ONCE

'Alan's on a train to Capital City,' Robin told Oluchi, ecstatic with relief. 'Gisborne had their whole house bugged, so they heard him speaking to me. His thugs wrecked their house and ordered Alan to leave town. But his mum is being super weird and he's got nowhere to go, so I've arranged to meet up with him.'

When Alan called, Robin had been in the middle of typing a message, asking his hacking guru D'Angela for ideas about the best way to trace the owner of the charging receipt. He typed the last line and sent this message before calling Will Scarlock. The rebel leader had only left the Nest minutes earlier, but the call went to his voicemail.

'Gonna run to the security office,' Robin said. 'I can be there in three minutes.'

'Where are you meeting Alan?' Oluchi asked.

Robin didn't answer because he jumped the entirety of the Nest's staircase, then set off across the casino at a sprint.

'I need transport!' Robin blurted as he charged into the security office. 'Tuxford station.'

Security chief Azeem, her sister Lyla and several other security officers were around a big oval conference table having their Monday morning strategy meeting. They didn't appreciate Robin's explosive entrance, but changed their tune once they understood what was going on.

Will Scarlock guessed where Robin would be and caught the end of his frantic explanation.

'Robin's not riding off on his own,' Will said. 'He needs a strong security escort.'

'Hold on,' Azeem said suspiciously. 'Isn't this all too convenient?'

Robin looked annoyed. 'What are you on about?'

'First thing this morning you get a call from Alan saying that Gisborne's people have got him. But somehow he managed to escape so that he could call you. Then Alan called you again, asking for you to meet him at a tiny village railway station halfway between Locksley and Nottingham.'

Will nodded thoughtfully, then looked at Robin. 'Who suggested Tuxford, you or Alan?'

'Alan, I guess,' Robin admitted. 'He might have nowhere to go when he reaches Capital City, so I asked him where his train was stopping. He read station names off the map inside the carriage. Alan said Tuxford was a good place to get off because he's been to some restaurant there with his parents and he reckons there's never anyone around.'

'What if this is a Gisborne ploy to lure Robin out of the forest and catch him?' Azeem asked.

'It's not.' Robin groaned. 'Alan's my friend. I trust him and I already promised to meet him at Tuxford. He also nabbed his dad's laptop. Nick Adale has been working alongside Gisborne for years, so if I can hack that laptop there could be all kinds of evidence about his dodgy dealings.'

'Robin, it's not a question of whether your friend is a decent person,' Lyla Masri pointed out firmly. 'The question is, what would Alan be prepared to do if Gisborne's thugs threatened to hurt him or a member of his family?'

'Even if it's not a trap, Gisborne might be having Alan followed to make sure he leaves the area,' Azeem added.

'So, we leave Alan in the middle of nowhere?' Robin protested, then spun around towards the exit. 'If you're not gonna help, I'll grab a dirt bike and ride to Tuxford on my own.'

'Stop being so dramatic!' Will said, grasping Robin's hoodie and tugging him back. 'We won't abandon your friend, but Lyla and Azeem are right. We have to be cautious. We need a plan that enables us to get Alan out of danger, but also take precautions in case Gisborne has set a trap.'

'Does Robin need to go?' one of the other security officers asked. 'Gisborne has zero chance of snaring Robin if he's here at Sherwood Castle.'

Robin looked like his head was about to explode. 'No way I'm not going! Alan's my mate and I am not your prisoner.'

Will looked conflicted, but made a rapid decision. 'I think Alan will feel more comfortable if Robin is there, rather than being met by strangers.'

'Exactly,' Robin said, pleased that Will had taken his side.

'No time to waste,' Azeem said, standing up and taking charge of her team. 'I want three quad bikes fuelled and ready to leave in fifteen minutes. We'll need five experienced and well-armed officers, plus Robin. We'll need two vans ready when we get to our transit hub on the southern edge of the forest. Bring heat-sensitive cameras and a drone so we can scout the station and spot anyone Gisborne has hiding nearby.'

Will glanced at Robin as Azeem kept up the stream of orders for her security team. 'Where's your bow?' he asked.

Robin usually took his bow everywhere, but in School Zone weapons were banned.

'My bedroom in the penthouse.'

'Better go get it then,' Will urged. 'And you'll need boots, water, warm clothes and snacks in case you get stuck overnight.'

'Yes, Mummy,' Robin said cheekily, then turned back as he was halfway out of the door. 'Where are we meeting?'

'Rear courtyard by the fuel tanks,' Azeem said. 'Thirteen minutes.'

Robin gave Azeem a thumbs up before shooting out. He had to pass near School Zone to get to the stairs, and a bunch of kids, including Matt Maid, were in the hallway between classrooms. They were supposed to be doing pastel drawings, but were mostly messing around.

'Hood baby!' Matt blurted, then cracked a huge smile as he ran after Robin. 'Is it true you threw the big hole punch at Mr Khan?'

'It's so cool that you got expelled,' a girl running behind added. 'I heard there's blood all over the carpet in Khan's office.'

'You're a legend,' Matt continued. 'But I wouldn't want to be in your shoes when my mums find out.'

'Karma and Indio already found out,' Robin said irritably, as he dodged Matt and kept running.

Twelve floors up to the penthouse left Robin breathless, and he was grateful there were no adults he needed to explain himself to when he got there. He took water, M&Ms and beef jerky from the kitchen, went to his bedroom for his bow, packed his grubby forest pack with plenty of arrows and buzzed with excitement as he donned thick clothes, hiking boots and a crash helmet for the muddy ride through the forest.

Robin considered Azeem's theory that Alan was the bait in a trap as he ran back downstairs. After making a diversion and crossing the third floor to avoid another encounter with School Zone, Robin felt his phone vibrate inside his thick combat trousers as he headed for the courtyard out back.

'This is Tybalt Bull,' the guy on the other end said. 'Is it safe to talk?'

Robin was thinking of six things at once and took a second to remember who Tybalt even was.

'You're my dad's lawyer,' Robin said, as he jogged. 'This call is untraceable and encrypted at my end, but I'm in a massive hurry right now.'

'There are some matters I need to discuss with you regarding parental custody and your father's appeal,' Tybalt explained rapidly. 'The appeal court judge could review your father's case any day now and since you witnessed the events that led to your father's imprisonment, I'd like you to come by my office and make a statement.'

Robin laughed. 'You know I can't exactly go wandering into Locksley?'

'Obviously,' Tybalt said. 'I've already discussed security arrangements with Emma Scarlock. If you're agreeable, I have an office set up where we can meet this evening at seven.'

'I guess that'll work,' Robin said.

Robin used his shoulder to barge through double doors and his sweaty skin caught a blast of cold air as he stepped into the gravel lot at the rear of the castle. There were three two-seater quad bikes ready to roll and a bunch of rebels loading equipment.

Lyla Masri shouted at Robin. 'You're last to arrive, move it!'

'I have to go,' Robin told Tybalt as he jumped down three steps into the parking lot. 'See you tonight, I guess.'

'I'll liaise with Emma for the final arrangements,' Tybalt agreed, as Robin ended the call.

Robin zipped his phone inside his pack, because things fall out of pockets on bumpy quad bike rides.

'You're in the middle quad with me,' Lyla told Robin as he reached the quads.

'Can I drive?' Robin asked keenly.

'In your dreams, buddy.' Lyla snorted, then looked concerned when she saw Robin's expression. 'You OK? You look worried.'

Robin shrugged and shook his head. 'Just stressed,' he answered. 'It's all happening today.'

21. IT'S A TRAP

Robin was a thrill-seeker. Although he didn't get to drive, he loved charging through the forest with his arms around Lyla's waist, getting thrown around in his seat, lashed by branches and sprayed with water as the trio of quad bikes blasted along a shallow tributary of the Macondo River.

The rebels kept a small fleet of road-legal vehicles in an abandoned grain silo at the forest's edge. With the increasing threats from bandits, the silo had two permanent guards. After a quick exchange of hugs and hellos, the rebels transferred their gear from the three quad bikes to a pair of decrepit white panel vans, marked with the faded logos of an electrical installation company.

The next stretch of the journey was all winding country roads. Hilly grasslands beyond hedgerows were dotted with cows and sheep, and the only sign of the troubles in nearby Locksley and Sherwood Forest were houses with barred windows and the logos of private security companies on tall wire fences.

'Spent a weekend in a tent with my dad around here,' Robin said, as they passed a waterlogged campsite with a *Closed for Winter* sign.

He was in the middle seat of the lead van, with Lyla driving and Ísbjörg on the passenger side. When the sat-nav showed they were two kilometres from the village of Tuxford, Robin slid a tiny stealth drone out of a plastic storage container.

He used an app to program in Tuxford station's exact location, then passed the drone to Ísbjörg and snapped on a set of first-person view (FPV) goggles.

'Gotta slow to fifteen kilometres per hour for launch,' Robin told Lyla.

As the van slowed down, Ísbjörg opened the passenger-side window and balanced the drone in the palm of her hand. After waiting to clear a bunch of overhanging trees she told Robin to launch.

He felt disorientated, his eyes seeing the view through the flying drone's front camera, while his body felt the van accelerate along the twisty road.

The stealth drone was no larger than a sparrow and designed to emit one tenth the noise of a buzzing hobbyist drone. With the destination programmed in, Robin only had to watch as the drone used terrain mapping to skim over treetops and stay out of sight.

He felt nervous when the drone stopped to hover less than a metre above the ground at the edge of the railway tracks a hundred metres south of Tuxford station's single platform. Robin used his smartphone to set the drone's camera to record at its highest resolution and frame rate, then flipped steering to manual and sent it towards the platform at maximum acceleration.

The drone was small and quiet, but not invisible. The idea was to skim the length of the platform once at top speed, fast enough that the drone would be gone before anyone knew what they'd seen.

The high-speed flyover took less than five seconds – too fast for Robin to see anything but a blur through the goggles. He set the drone to return to the van, rested the goggles on top of his head, then replayed the footage in slow motion on his phone.

'It's nicely done up,' Robin noted, as his screen showed Tuxford station's single central platform with immaculately painted signs, lavish flower beds that spelled out the station's name, and a wooden shelter festooned with plants in hanging baskets.

'I guess the locals look after it,' Ísbjörg said. 'Tuxford is well snobby. All rip-off antique shops and pubs that charge thirty quid for a cheeseburger with a few strings of grated truffle.'

Robin moved the footage on to the point where the drone filmed Alan from above. His friend sat on a white bench next to his wheeled case. His posture seemed anxious and he gripped his phone tightly.

'Should I call him?' Robin asked.

'Why let anyone know we're coming?' Lyla asked. 'We'll be there soon.'

Everything looked good until Robin got to the last second of the recording.

Since tracks ran on either side of Tuxford's single platform, passengers were supposed to wait for a green signal light and walk across a train track to leave the station. But at the far end where the platform sloped down to meet the track bed, Robin noticed two sets of boot prints in the soft ground.

Living in the forest had taught Robin that tracks fill with moisture and soften as they age, but these prints were crisp and had almost certainly been made since Alan arrived.

'Couple of people have been sneaking around in the mud at the end of the platform,' Robin told Lyla, as he zoomed in on the prints. 'Maybe you were right about Gisborne keeping eyes on Alan.'

Ísbjörg craned her neck to see Robin's screen and nodded. 'Passengers have no reason to walk down there. It has to be someone watching Alan.'

'Life's never simple,' Robin moaned.

Lyla parked the van by a wooden fence a few hundred metres outside of Tuxford Village's main drag. The second van parked behind and Robin and the five rebel security officers discussed strategy as they peeled off muddy outer layers, so they didn't stick out walking around the upscale village.

'I say we split into three groups,' Lyla decided. 'Keep our earpieces in and let everyone know the instant you see something.'

She pointed at Jules, Zenith and Laing, the three rebels who'd ridden in the second van.

'Jules, park your van directly in front of Tuxford station. Let us know if you see anything suspicious and keep the engine running in case we need to leave in a hurry. Zenith, you ride to the station with Jules. Hide a big gun under your coat and take some smoke grenades in case things turn nasty. When you get to the station buy a ticket from the machine, then go onto the platform. Stand close to Alan, but don't speak to him.

'I'll team up with Laing and sweep briskly along the tracks from south of the platform. We'll use the heat-sensitive camera to see if any of Gisborne's people are hiding nearby. Robin and Ísbjörg will approach from the north and do the same.'

'There were two distinct sets of boot prints in that drone footage,' Ísbjörg added. 'Be careful, because the bad guys may have split up.'

'How about I put the drone back up?' Robin suggested, as he swapped his chunky forest boots for a cleanish pair of Converse All Stars. 'If I set it to hover at a hundred metres, it'll stay airborne for fifteen minutes. We'll get a bird's-eye view over the whole station and you won't see or hear it at that height.'

'Good idea,' Lyla agreed. 'But the longer we wait around here, the more chance there is we'll get spotted. So, does everyone know exactly what they're supposed to be doing?'

Robin and the five security officers nodded and said yes.

'Check your earpiece radios,' Lyla said. 'Then let's get to work.'

22. HANGING BASKET CASES

They'd checked the timetables, so Robin crept through bushes onto the tracks north of Tuxford station, knowing there was no train scheduled for twenty-two minutes.

He quickly pulled down the FPV goggles to make sure there was nothing to see from the hovering drone, while Ísbjörg scanned back and forth with a heat camera. It was sensitive enough to detect any living thing, or even residual heat from someone who'd disturbed the ground minutes earlier.

'All I see are rats nesting under the platform,' Ísbjörg told Robin reassuringly.

After their initial checks the pair moved along the tracks swiftly because they were out in the open. An all-clear report came from Lyla and Laing to the south, and Zenith radioed in to say he was now on the station platform less than five metres from Alan.

Robin tensed up as he reached the area with the boot prints. It hadn't been possible to tell the size of the prints from the drone footage, and he was surprised to realise that they were no bigger than his own.

'Kinda small for Gisborne's thugs,' Robin said, confused. 'Though he uses women too.'

'No trace,' Ísbjörg said, as she leaned out along one side of the platform with the heat detector. 'Whoever made those boot prints hasn't been back since the first drone flight.'

Robin checked the image from the drone and saw nothing again. When he pulled the goggles away, he got a fleeting glance of Laing's bulky frame peering down the tracks from the opposite side of the platform.

'No signs of life at this end,' Lyla told her earpiece radio. Then Ísbjörg, Jules and Zen also gave the all-clear. 'Stay cautious. Let's get Alan.'

'I'll cover with my bow,' Robin said. Ísbjörg walked up the ramp onto the platform and Zenith glanced around furtively before sitting on the bench next to Alan.

As Robin notched an arrow in his bow, he watched Zenith calmly tell Alan that he was here with Robin and that they were going to walk to the front of the station, where he'd find a white van with the engine running.

Alan asked suspiciously, 'Where's Robin?' but Robin didn't see what his oldest friend did next because a figure darted in from bushes at the side of the tracks.

Robin spun around to aim his bow, but the small, squat figure swung a long-handled garden hoe, which clanked against the FPV goggles on Robin's head and sent him stumbling backwards.

'Guys!' Robin shouted, as he landed awkwardly on top of his bow and a piece of railway track.

'I know who you are!' the person with the hoe shouted.

Robin rolled over and was relieved to see that, rather than one of Guy Gisborne's oversized goons, his enemy was a robust elderly lady in a well-worn gardener's overall.

'You should be in school!' the woman continued, as she clattered Robin with the hoe again. 'You're the little yob who pulled up the spring bulbs I planted and threw my hanging baskets onto the tracks.'

'I've never been here before,' Robin protested, holding his hands over his face as he realised that the first blow with the hoe had cracked the FPV goggles.

At the same time a second figure came across the track. He was a boy of about eleven who bore a family resemblance to the hoe-wielding nutter.

'Nanny, that can't be the kid who's been vandalising the station,' the kid blurted. 'That's Robin Hood!'

The kid tried to grab the hoe from his grandmother and Robin tried to roll away, but he still caught a third mighty whack across the thigh.

'I don't care what his name is,' the mad granny continued. 'I know it's him who wrecked my hanging baskets.'

'Leave me alone,' Robin begged, just as he realised that the woman and her grandson's gardening boots were a perfect match for the smallish prints in the mud.

The woman finally stopped swinging when Ísbjörg and Lyla arrived at the end of the platform and ordered her to calm down.

'And what are all you lot doing at my station?' she asked suspiciously.

Her grandson looked embarrassed and snatched the hoe off his nan in case she kicked off again. A hundred metres up, the tiny drone detected that it had lost the signal from the FPV goggles and made a neat emergency landing on the platform.

Robin's thigh hurt and he had a cut on his head where the edge of the hoe caught him, but the main injury was to his pride. He forgot all his aches when he saw that Alan had ignored the instruction to walk to the waiting van. His friend now stood between Ísbjörg and Lyla at the end of the platform.

'OK, mate?' Robin asked, as he stepped onto the platform. He teared up as he pulled his oldest friend into a tight hug.

'I've been feeling like crap,' Alan admitted as tears streaked his cheeks. 'But getting rescued and seeing an old lady batter you with a garden tool has cheered me up.'

'I've missed your abuse,' Robin joked, as he stepped back, rubbed one wet eye and whacked Alan fondly on the shoulder.

'You get to be a rebel like me now!' he continued. 'I've got a sweet room in the penthouse, and you can see the Nest, where I've got the most outrageous hacking set-up. And you can meet my girl Josie and all the other cool people at Sherwood Castle.'

Everyone enjoyed watching the friends reunite, but Lyla hurried them up. 'You can chat all you like once we're on the road. But there's still a chance Gisborne has someone watching this area, so let's get out of here.'

'One second!' the grandson begged, as he stepped up onto the platform holding his phone. 'I'm sorry my nan clobbered you, Robin, but can I get a selfie? Nobody in my class will believe I met Robin Hood if I don't.'

'Do you get this everywhere you go?' Alan asked, shaking his head wryly.

Robin nodded as he put an arm around the kid's back and grinned for the selfie. 'I'm basically a superstar now.'

Ísbjörg rolled her eyes. 'You certainly have a superstar-sized ego.'

Lyla gave the starstruck grandson a finger wag and a stern warning. 'Don't share that selfie with anyone until we've had a full hour to clear out of this area. Unless you want me to come back and pay you a visit.'

23. WORLDS COLLIDE

Alan was an extra body for the return to Sherwood Castle, so they took a fourth quad bike after dropping the vans back at the grain silo. Robin got to drive, with Alan as his passenger.

As a kid from one of Locksley's richest suburbs, Alan was wary. He'd grown up hearing TV news stories that portrayed Sherwood Forest as wildly dangerous, and hearing privileged adults in his parents' social circle who spoke about Forest People as if they were barely human creatures who stole mobile phones and hijacked cars at gunpoint.

'Don't sweat,' Robin told his friend as he got off the quad bike, touched his head and realised it was still bleeding. 'You'll be fine.'

He'd parked in front of Sherwood Castle's main foyer which, despite major damage in the summer floods, still looked like the entrance of a five-star resort. Alan eyed the armed security officer by the revolving doors, while the people coming in and out wearing combat gear and mud-caked boots made his sneakers and yellow tracksuit stick out.

The lobby felt wonderfully warm after the long ride. The giant glass aquarium behind the hotel reception now only housed a sinister collection of fish skeletons, while the reception desks where hotel guests checked in had been turned into a security checkpoint, with bag searches and metal detectors.

Alan joined the back of a short queue, but Lyla let them through a staff door at the side.

'Can I check my phone now?' Alan asked keenly, as they stepped into what had originally been the hotel manager's office. 'My mum might have answered my messages.'

Robin shook his head. 'The instant your phone goes live, your location can be tracked. You have to leave it in airplane mode until I can sort you some location-masking software. Now we'll grab a quick bite, then go to the Nest where I can start having a go at cracking your dad's laptop.'

'I'll bet my dad's log-in is Mummysboy1971,' Alan said. 'He uses that password for everything.'

'My life will be easier if you're right.' Robin grinned as he headed out of the office.

But Lyla blocked Robin off.

'You're not rushing off to the Nest,' she said, as she gave Robin a look of concern. 'Go to the clinic to get that cut on your head checked out.'

'It barely hurts,' Robin protested.

Lyla tutted. 'It's still bleeding. I doubt it's serious, but better safe than sorry.'

Robin was annoyed because you always waited ages in the clinic and he was keen to show Alan around the castle and introduce him to Josie and the Maid family.

'Suppose you're right,' Robin said to Lyla. 'Can you at least get someone to take Nick Adale's laptop up to the Nest for me? Oluchi can start looking at it.'

The clinic was a five-minute walk past the castle's indoor pool, but Robin hadn't eaten since breakfast so he diverted through the colony of food outlets around the fountains in the resort's main atrium.

They originally sold fancy cakes and overpriced sandwiches to affluent resort guests, but the four units reopened by Forest People now served cheap meals to rebels and refugees.

Robin's favourite was a former champagne bar, lavishly decorated with black marble and gold leaf, where a cheerful couple served up Italian food. He bought two homemade lemonades, two giant tubs of spaghetti with meatballs and a stick of ciabatta bread to mop up the sauce.

'Good?' Robin asked, as the boys walked and scoffed out of paper trays.

'Really good,' Alan agreed as he dropped some spaghetti on the floor. 'This isn't how I imagined you living.'

'What did you imagine?'

Alan looked embarrassed as they exited the atrium into a broad hallway with a marble floor and chandeliers. 'I thought you'd all be huddled up under animal skins, making protest banners, while snot-nosed kids ran around with no shoes. I definitely didn't imagine a heated pool and fresh baked bread.'

Robin laughed. 'There are a lot of desperate people in the forest. We had no heat or light here through the coldest part of winter, but it's almost civilised now we've got a mains electricity hook-up. Even the elevators work, though I've got stuck twice so I stick to the stairs.'

The rebels' brightly lit medical clinic also impressed as Alan entered. The space had originally been a small exhibition hall but, thanks to donations from the billionaire owner of online shopping site TwoTu, it bristled with modern hospital-white equipment, including an MRI scanner, a dental suite, a basic operating theatre and three private suites for forest women to give birth.

Apparently four on a Monday afternoon was a good time to get injured, because there was only one other person in the waiting area. Robin just had time to text Josie saying where he was and install a location-masking app on Alan's phone.

'Guess what?' Alan said bitterly after checking his messages. 'Not a squeak out of my mum. Me and Dakota could be dead for all that woman cares.'

'Sorry to hear that, mate,' Robin said, but before he could offer more sympathy, eighty-five-year-old Dr Gladys came charging towards them.

The clinic had nurses and assistants to deal with minor injuries, so Robin knew that the feisty little doctor had more than his cut head on her mind.

'What are you keeping me busy with now, Robin Hood?' Dr Gladys asked furiously as she put a battered leather medical bag down on the seat next to him. 'I spent most of Saturday night extracting your arrow from a bandit's ankle. And this morning that lovely Mr Khan needed stitches after you threw a hole punch at him.'

Alan didn't know who Mr Khan was, so he looked baffled as the scowling doctor pulled a disposable glove over her tiny, wrinkled hand, then flicked the cut on Robin's head.

'Oww!' Robin protested.

'Stop being a wimp,' Dr Gladys ordered, then took a little aerosol and blasted it around the cut.

'Cold!' Robin gasped as the icy spray congealed and one streak ran down his neck and inside his shirt.

'Nothing worth stitching,' the doctor said, as she gave Robin the little spray can. 'The scalp is thin and has lots of blood vessels, so even a small cut on the head can bleed profusely. Give that hair a scrub to get all the mud out, then dry the wound gently and give it another good blast with this disinfectant spray.'

'Thank you, doctor,' Robin said politely, then whispered to Alan as she walked away. 'Old ladies seem to have it in for me today.'

As the boys headed for the exit, Robin incurred Dr Gladys' wrath once again.

'And I suppose you're going to leave those spaghetti trays under my waiting room chairs?'

As Robin sheepishly picked up his litter, Josie charged in. She had a huge grin as she slapped Robin on the back.

'Way to get expelled from school, ya big idiot,' Josie said, then turned to Alan. 'You must be the bestest friend I've heard so much about.'

'Hi,' Alan said to Josie, then looked at Robin. 'You got expelled? I didn't even realise you had school here.'

'Robin doesn't,' Josie said cheerfully.

'They'll let me back in,' Robin dismissed her. 'I'll probably have to do a whole bunch of *yes-sir no-sirs* and write some stupid apology.'

'If you say so,' Josie answered. 'You've got to invite me to dinner in the penthouse tonight. I need to be there when Karma and Indio yell at you.'

'Already eaten,' Robin said, acting annoyed but secretly loving the attention Josie was giving him. 'I've got to wash out the cut on my head, then I've got to go to the Nest and see how Oluchi's getting on with her investigations. Then I've got to go back across the forest later for some meeting with my dad's lawyer in Locksley.'

'Shame,' Josie grunted as they walked out of the clinic and headed under a big *CASINO* sign and up a dead escalator towards the Nest. 'But Alan, you've known Robin his whole life – what's the number-one most embarrassing thing you can tell me about him?'

24. IT WAS MUD, DAMMIT

'Robin was about nine,' Alan told Josie as they walked across the thick casino carpet towards the Nest with Robin a few steps behind. 'Parents signed us up for this mini-rugby week to get us off their backs during Easter hols. And you know how rugby has the big H-shaped post that you kick the ball through?'

'Of course,' Josie said. 'Did Robin smash into it?'

'Better than that,' Alan said, smirking. 'They'd taken one post away to be repaired. So, Robin was running with the ball and his front foot goes straight down the hole. The hole's full of water. It all squirts up in his face and he's all twisted up with his leg wedged in the hole.

'The rugby coach came running over and lifted Robin out, but the best part was, falling down the hole gave Robin such a fright that he shat his shorts.'

'Seriously?' Josie said, howling with laughter.

'It was running down his legs . . .'

'You're full of it,' Robin said, tutting and sounding defensive. 'My whole foot would never have fitted down that hole when I was nine. We were five years old and the stuff running down my legs was muddy water.'

'I'm sticking to my version of the story,' Alan said, as Josie kept laughing. 'All the older kids were killing themselves laughing and calling Robin *Crap Legs*. I had to sit next to him on the bus home and he smelled *so* bad!'

Robin pretended to sulk as they got close to the Nest, but though the jokes were at his expense, he enjoyed hanging out with Alan for the first time in almost a year and seeing Josie laugh.

'You're both totally immature,' Robin said, as he took a short run-up and gave Josie a gentle kick up the bum. She didn't retaliate because they'd reached the door at the back of the casino.

'You been here all day?' Robin asked Oluchi as he reached the top of the stairs and entered the Nest.

The young journalist looked bleary-eyed, and had notebooks, Post-its and dead coffees littering her workstation. As Alan got his first look at the Nest and admired the rows of spinning fans at the back of the bright green supercomputer, Robin noticed his hacking guru D'Angela in a chat window on Oluchi's screen and gave her a wave.

'Good to see you!' Robin told her brightly then, after introducing Josie and Alan, 'Have we made progress?'

'Oluchi's doing a great job,' D'Angela said.

'The image search you've been running on the Super found a match for Heirani Stone,' Oluchi began. 'Her original name was Heirani Amo. She was twenty-two, from a boatload of refugees who arrived in Sherwood after the tsunami in French Polynesia. D'Angela's crew has also hacked the account linked to the car charging receipt. It belonged to Heirani's older brother, Max Amo.'

'That's definitely her,' Alan said, a lump swelling in his throat as he looked at one of Oluchi's printouts and saw the face from his nightmares. 'She was burned and bloody, but it's the girl I saw thrown into the car.'

'Max probably died in the explosion too,' Oluchi continued. 'We found a social media account where Max was posting several times per day. He hasn't logged in since the explosion and a couple of guys have posted comments, asking why he didn't show at a party at Locksley University on Saturday night.'

'Anything on the third victim?' Robin asked. 'Or the whereabouts of Max's car?'

'Still working on that,' Oluchi said. 'But Lyla brought Nick Adale's laptop up here, so we've been concentrating on that for the past half hour.'

'Anything good so far?' Alan asked hopefully.

'You gave us the right password,' Oluchi told Alan. 'There are hundreds of messages between Gisborne and your dad, which will take time to read through. But the standout thing is emails your dad sent to a woman named Katerina Kendall.'

'I know that name,' Alan said. 'When Gisborne called on Saturday evening, my dad asked why he was being sent to deal with a waste management problem instead of Kendall.'

D'Angela spoke on screen. 'Nick Adale sent some furious emails to Katerina Kendall on Sunday, accusing her of dropping him in it and saying that he's sick of clearing up problems that her department created.

'Katerina Kendall has an office in Locksley, but she looks after her elderly father and mostly works from home. If you really want to know about the dodgy stuff that Gisborne Waste Management gets up to, we need to hack Kendall. And since any sensible criminal doesn't leave too many traces in emails and official documents, we need to know what she's saying.'

Robin nodded. 'You mean bug her house?'

'I got rumbled because Gisborne had our house bugged,' Alan pointed out. 'Gisborne will have Kendall's house bugged too, so they'll hear if we try to break in.'

'We'll have to be careful,' Oluchi agreed. 'But D'Angela thinks we can bug the house without going inside.'

'So, we've found Kendall's address?' Robin asked.

'It's a bungalow,' Oluchi said. 'It's on a large plot of land in a near-deserted neighbourhood on the western side of Locksley.'

'The easiest way to bug a house you don't want to get close to is with laser microphones,' D'Angela added. 'The laser beam is invisible and can detect minute vibrations in glass when someone speaks. Point one at a window from up to a hundred metres away, and you can hear every word spoken inside.'

Robin scoffed. 'Do we happen to have a couple of laser microphones lying around?'

'No,' D'Angela said. 'But you've got loads of money from the Mindy Burger robbery and I know a company that can get them delivered by express courier in under two hours.'

Robin tutted. 'Great, I'm paying for them . . . How much?'

'A good pair of laser microphones costs about five thousand,' D'Angela said. 'Then all we need to do is find someone who can set them up. Laser microphones can be finicky, so it has to be someone who's good with technology.'

'Someone small and fast,' Oluchi added, as she grinned at Robin. 'Someone who would feel confident scouting a location, then shimmying up a telephone pole, or walking across the roof of an abandoned house in the dark—'

Josie looked at Alan and cracked a big grin before she interrupted. 'Bring spare underwear in case he falls down any holes . . .'

25. SIGN HERE

Josie's grumpy dad called, telling her to get home for dinner and homework. Robin took Alan up to the penthouse and introduced him to Karma, Indio and the rest of the Maid family.

This currently included baby Zack, wearing a jar of apple puree, and Finn and Otto, who were belting each other with sofa cushions, while Matt and two of his school mates were supposed to be doing homework, but were mostly just wrestling and throwing soggy balls of paper off the balcony.

'You can stay with me for now,' Robin told Alan, as he stepped into his spacious room. 'There's a mattress under my bed that Marion used to sleep on. Help yourself to anything in the kitchen.'

'Great view,' Alan said, as he looked out of giant floor-to-ceiling windows as the sun set over Sherwood Forest.

'I wish I could hang out with you tonight, but I can't miss the meeting with my dad's lawyer.'

'Hopefully I'll crash,' Alan said, as he admired Robin's huge bed and poked his nose into the fancy marble bathroom. 'I've barely slept the past two nights.'

Robin sensed Alan's unease as his friend slumped in a chair by the window.

'You'll be OK here,' Robin said.

Alan sighed. 'Everyone seems nice but I feel really anxious. I don't know if Dakota's safe, or what happened when my dad met Gisborne.'

'Did you try to contact them?'

'Dad hasn't replied to the message I sent, which is no surprise since he thinks I betrayed him. Dakota got a phone when she started at Locksley High, but she smashed her first one and lost the second. Now Dad says she can't have a phone until she learns to look after her stuff.'

'Oluchi thinks they'll both be OK, at least while Gisborne is running for sheriff,' Robin said. 'And because your mum has an important job down in Capital City.'

Alan thumped both arms of his chair and tried to explain his frustration. 'It's like I've lived my whole life one way. Then everything got ripped apart in three days.'

Robin smiled. 'That sounds *very* familiar. When the rebels rescued me a year ago, my dad had been thrown in jail and I had no idea where Little John had disappeared to.'

'Can I use your bath?' Alan asked. 'I'm grubby from the quad bike and a soak might help me to chill out.'

'Makes sense,' Robin said. 'I'll start your bath while I shower and clean my cut. I hate baths, but you can go ask Karma or Indio. They have bath salts and fancy oils. Or there's Baby Shark bubble bath for your inner child.'

Ten minutes later, Alan was checking the temperature of his bath water while Robin stood in front of his mirror in shorts and a T-shirt, gently towelling his hair to avoid reopening his cut.

'Play music if you like,' Robin told his friend. 'There's a wireless speaker on the shelf. Press and hold the red button on top to pair it with your phone.'

'For sure,' Alan said, as the penthouse doorbell chimed.

Three-year-old Finn opened the giant door, yelled, 'You can't come in!' then ran off squealing with laughter.

'Finn, don't be cheeky,' Indio said, stepping into the hallway as Robin peeked out of his room and saw Emma Scarlock and Mr Khan with a giant dressing above one eye.

'Oh balls!' Robin gasped, as he frantically picked socks and trousers off the floor. 'I don't need this now . . .'

Alan leaned out of the bathroom with no shirt on. 'What's up?'

'I'm gonna get a long lecture from four grown-ups if I stick around,' Robin explained, as he pulled on the trousers and scooped up a backpack, coat and boots.

'You'll have to face them eventually,' Alan pointed out.

'But not tonight,' Robin said, as he took another peek into the hallway. 'I'm knackered.'

Robin was pleased to see Indio leading Mr Khan and Emma Scarlock out of the hallway and into the living room.

'When Sheriff Marjorie built this place, she had an escape hatch put in,' Robin explained, stuffing his laptop and some other gear down his backpack 'There's a hole behind the wardrobe in the middle bedroom. If anyone asks, I left five minutes ago.'

Alan wasn't comfortable lying to adults he'd only just met. 'I'm locking the door, turning up the music and getting in the bath.'

Robin decided it was safest to leave now and put his socks, jacket and boots on after he'd escaped into the service corridor. He hopped out into the hallway with his stuff bundled in his arms and shot towards the door of the middle bedroom, which was shared by Matt, Otto and Finn.

'Good evening,' Will Scarlock said loudly from behind.

Robin dropped half his stuff and spun around to see Will entering through the main door.

'Hey,' Robin said weakly.

'Robin Hood couldn't possibly be trying to sneak out,' Will said sarcastically. 'Because I *know* he's a better person than that.'

'I . . .' Robin spluttered, picking up the balled socks that had rolled across the floor. 'Just putting my dirty gear in the laundry room.'

This lie didn't hold up because Robin wore boots and a backpack. Indio was even less impressed by Robin's half-assed escape attempt as she came out of the living room to greet Will.

'Dress fast and get in the living room,' she growled.

'I have to meet Tybalt in town.' Robin squirmed.

'We know you do,' Will said. 'I've arranged transport – for *after* this discussion about your education.'

Robin felt defeated. He moaned to Alan while he got dressed in his room, then scowled at the floor as he crossed the hallway. One living-room chair had been set in front of the huge fireplace for Robin. Mr Khan, Will, Emma and Karma sat on a pair of sofas facing him, and Indio joined the line-up after shooing away Finn and Matt, who were trying to listen at the door.

After an awkward silence, Robin spoke first. 'Get it over with, then. Gang up and tell me what a terrible person I am.'

Mr Khan shot to his feet and gesticulated with both arms. 'There, you see?' he howled. 'That's Robin's attitude. He thinks school is a joke and shows adults zero respect.'

To Robin's surprise, Indio snapped back at Mr Khan. 'In Robin's defence, the call he tried to answer was from his friend. Alan would now be alone in the dark, wandering dangerous Capital City streets if Robin hadn't helped.'

Karma looked at Mr Khan and backed up her partner. 'Sometimes a little flexibility and common sense does no harm.'

Robin fought the urge to grin as Mr Khan pointed at the dressing over his eye. 'I can't have this!' he roared.

'My teaching staff work long hours for no money. *Every* pupil must stick to the same rules and show respect. The other kids can't see special treatment for the famous Robin Hood.'

Emma Scarlock stood up, put herself between the two sofas and tried to sound diplomatic. 'I thought we had an agreement to present a united front now that Robin is here,' she began. 'School Zone will implement a new policy where pupils can leave their phone on, but only if they notify staff that they are expecting an urgent call.'

'Strictly in exceptional circumstances,' Mr Khan added grudgingly. 'Not every time Robin decides something is important.'

'Of course.' Karma nodded, then looked sternly at Robin. 'This morning's incident was regrettable, but I'm more concerned with Robin skipping lessons and not doing his homework.'

'I'm not that bad,' Robin said. 'Some of the forest kids are way worse.'

'Forest kids don't live in a penthouse with electric light and hot water,' Mr Khan pointed out. 'It's not a fair comparison.'

Emma spoke next. 'We've agreed that you can return to School Zone, but only if you sign a good behaviour contract and stick to it like glue.'

The other adults murmured in agreement as Emma Scarlock took a piece of paper out of a small backpack and handed it to Robin.

'Let's hear it,' Will said. 'The whole thing, out loud.'

Robin sighed as he read from the sheet. 'Number one, I, Robin Hood, agree to switch my phone off and hand it to my teacher at the start of every lesson, unless I get permission to do otherwise.

'Number two, I will catch up with all of my missing homework over the next two weeks.

'Number three, I will hand all new homework in on time.

'Number four, I will not skip any lessons without permission.

'Number five, I will show a positive attitude in class and not mess around.

'Number six, to show my appreciation for the hard work done by volunteer teaching staff, including Mr Khan, I will stay for one hour each day after school. I will wipe tables, vacuum the carpet tiles and perform other general cleaning tasks.

'Number seven, I agree to do this cleaning every day after school until I have caught up with all my homework, completed one full school term without missing any lessons, handed all new homework in promptly, and demonstrated excellent behaviour in class at all times.'

Robin looked miserable as he lowered the sheet of paper. Mr Khan enjoyed this and cracked a giant smile as he reached into his jacket for a gold fountain pen.

'We're not messing around, Robin,' Indio said firmly. 'Karma and I love you and treat you the same as our biological children. But you're not an adult. You don't get to make your own rules.'

Robin felt conflicted. His inner renegade wanted to remind the grown-ups about all the stuff he'd done to help the rebel movement, then tell them where to stick their good behaviour contract and storm out.

But Indio and Karma had stuck up for him, which meant a lot. And though School Zone was mostly tedious, he'd miss hanging out with Josie and his other friends.

Robin sighed. 'The only problem with this contract is that I help Sheila with the chickens after school.'

'We spoke to Sheila already,' Emma answered. 'She's happy for you to go to the chicken sheds before school instead.'

'You've thought of everything . . .' Robin groaned.

He realised how tired he was going to be, getting up early to help with the chickens, a full day in School Zone, then cleaning up for an hour after, checking surveillance in the Nest, then doing new homework, plus old homework that he'd missed.

At least my Vietnamese essay-writing friend can help, he thought sneakily.

Mr Khan looked irritated by Robin's hesitation.

Will wasn't impressed either. 'This isn't a negotiation,' he told Robin firmly.

'Fine,' Robin said as he took Mr Khan's pen, rested the behaviour contract on his knee and signed his name. 'Let's get this over with . . .'

26. BRAIN ACHE

Two hours later, Robin was hiding in the trunk of a rebel car as it thumped into one of the many potholes on Locksley's crumbling roads.

'Careful!' Robin ranted, as he protected the cut on his head with one hand. 'And it smells like arse back here. Maybe someday, someone could clean out a trunk before I have to ride in it.'

'But then you'd have one less thing to whinge about,' Neo Scarlock yelled back from the driving seat, as the car hit another spine-jarring bump. 'And we've arrived anyway.'

Neo pulled up at the blackened façade of an old brick office building. He pushed the button to open an electric tailgate and Robin stepped into the drizzly evening.

'Remember the entry code?' Neo asked, as Robin grabbed his backpack.

'Seven, six, two, four,' Robin said.

'Call me when you need your pickup,' Neo said. 'I'm heading to the Begonia Bar two blocks over. Monday night is half-price cocktails, and my brother says it's usually heaving with student girls.'

'Sounds like more fun than where I'm going,' Robin answered. 'And you're driving me back, so easy on the margaritas.'

As his battered ride drove off, Robin jogged down a narrow alley at the side of the office building and tapped 7624 into a keypad next to a rotting wooden door.

The back stairs of the old brick office building smelled of damp and mould as he raced up to the fifth floor, then started down a creepy unlit hallway with offices on either side.

Each office had the name of a lawyer or legal practice painted on frosted glass in the doors, but floor tiles were rotting and the offices Robin could see into looked like nobody had worked there in decades.

'Great, you made it,' a legal clerk in a dark suit said, as Robin stepped through a door with squealing hinges.

The smell of dust made Robin want to sneeze. He scanned a large store room lined with hundreds of rusting filing cabinets. The lighting flickered and a spinning ceiling fan wobbled and clanked, out of balance because one blade was missing.

'I'll text Tybalt so he knows you're here,' the clerk continued, sounding hurried. 'Unfortunately, he's got a meeting with Judge Intintola. He always runs late so you may have to wait a while. I got a sandwich, cake and cola from the courthouse café in case you were peckish.'

'Thank you,' Robin said, then sneezed twice.

'I have to get these documents back to a client,' the clerk said, before scooping a laptop, a coffee and a mountain of court papers off a leather-topped desk. 'And I almost forgot – an express delivery came to our main office.'

Robin was intrigued by the yellow package on the desk, but the clerk needed help getting through the door with his paper stack. After holding the door, Robin crossed the room and peeked out. The windows hadn't been cleaned in years, but he saw enough to realise that he was behind Locksley's modern glass court building on Civic Square.

The old wood and leather chair creaked dramatically as Robin settled behind the desk. He opened the can of Rage Cola, but realised he'd need to be fifty times hungrier to go near the squashed cheese-and-pickle sandwich and a muffin that looked as appetising as a house brick.

There was a satisfying shower of mud flakes as Robin thumped his boots on the desktop. Then he pulled out his folding knife, grabbed the bright yellow express delivery package and slashed it open.

'You don't get much for five thousand quid these days,' Robin told himself as he stripped away two sheets of bubble wrap and tipped out two domed packages containing laser microphones.

D'Angela said laser microphones were tricky to set up, so Robin decided to learn how to use them now, rather than later when he'd be creeping around in the dark. There were no instructions inside the package, but there was a slip of paper with a download link.

But it was half past seven on one of the most hectic days of Robin's life. His brain was fried, and to make matters worse the safety notice on the first page of the instructions suggested that the author hadn't mastered English:

BIG WARNING!
VERY POWER LASER – DO NOT STARE ON ME
POSSIBLE CAUSE EYE HURT

Nothing from the instructions seemed to penetrate Robin's brain, and his eyes rolled shut as his body slid down the comfy old chair. The next thing he felt was a gentle shoulder squeeze.

'Ahoy there, sleeping beauty,' Tybalt Bull said cheerfully.

Robin took a second to remember where he was. He tried to speak, but the dusty room had left his throat feeling rough.

'Sorry,' Robin finally croaked, after two mouthfuls of Rage Cola and an eye rub. 'Today has been absolutely—'

Robin stopped mid-sentence because the clerk had stepped back into the room, along with his . . .

'Dad!' Robin blurted. 'How are you here?'

He was suddenly wide awake and so frantic and emotional that he thumped his knee on the underside of the desk as he scrambled up.

'Did you escape?' Robin asked, as tears filled his eyes.

The small, bearded Ardagh Hood wore the baggy blue tracksuit and white laceless plimsolls of a Pelican Island prisoner. He almost got knocked off his feet as Robin charged in and grasped him tight.

'He'd better not escape,' Tybalt joked as Robin hugged his dad. 'I've spent the past two weeks working on your father's appeal.'

'Goodness, you're all muscle!' Ardagh said, as his youngest son squeezed the air out of him. 'You must weigh half a ton.'

Robin was thrilled that his dad had noticed. 'There's a massive gym at Sherwood Castle,' Robin boasted. 'I do weights three times per week. Though I'm still waiting for my growth spurt.'

'Good things come in small packages,' Ardagh joked, his mellow tone a contrast to Robin's excitement. 'Just like your old man.'

'So, if you didn't escape?' Robin asked.

'As a medium-security prisoner, your father was temporarily released into the custody of his legal team to meet the judge and discuss his appeal case,' Tybalt explained. 'He's not allowed outside Locksley courthouse, but this building is linked by a basement tunnel so we're not breaking any rules.'

'Glad you're not in trouble,' Robin told his dad, as the clerk found a couple of dusty stacking chairs so that everyone could sit down. 'And it's amazing to see you.'

'Your Auntie Pauline says you have a girlfriend now,' Ardagh said as he sat down.

'Josie's really nice,' Robin said, nodding as he found a picture of her on his phone.

'I hope you're being careful,' Ardagh said. 'I'm not ready to be a grandfather.'

'Daaaaad!' Robin gasped, his face turning bright red. 'I'm thirteen. It's not that serious. And if you don't want grandbabies, it's Clare and Little John you should be worrying about.'

Ardagh laughed gently. 'And Will Scarlock's people at the castle are looking after you?'

'The castle penthouse is . . .' Robin almost said 'way nicer than our draughty old house in Locksley', but realised his dad might be offended. 'Comfortable.'

'And how goes your education?'

'School Zone at the castle is great,' Robin said, then struggled to keep eye contact as he told a lie. 'I've been getting good grades and stuff.'

'Well, that's a change for the better,' Ardagh said happily. 'You and your friend Alan were always causing mischief at Locksley High. Skipping out of lessons and never doing your homework.'

Robin swiftly changed the subject. 'Is your appeal coming along well?'

Ardagh looked at his lawyer. 'Tybalt knows better than I do.'

Tybalt nodded, then began an explanation as he sat on the edge of the desk. 'Your father was convicted on two matters. The first was the trumped-up charge of stealing laptops from Captain Cash. But my appeal is based on the second, more serious charge, that your father attacked two police officers who came to arrest him at your house.'

'The ones who left me with three broken bones and taser burns all over my body,' Ardagh added bitterly, before Tybalt continued.

'When a police officer claims that someone attacked them, they are supposed to gather evidence and write a detailed report about what happened. But the officers who took your father to Locksley Central Police Station didn't file any paperwork. They also had their body cameras switched off and claimed that the CCTV system at the police station was faulty on the day your dad was brought in.'

'Sounds well dodgy,' Robin said. 'But is that enough to get my dad out of prison?'

'I think we have a solid case,' Tybalt said. 'The appeal court judge has begun looking at our new evidence. Your father met the judge to answer some questions earlier today, and we should be called in to hear her final verdict within a month.'

'Aren't most judges around here friends of Gisborne, though?' Robin asked.

'Locksley judges are notoriously corrupt,' Tybalt agreed. 'Fortunately, appeal judges are sent from other parts of the country to review cases. I get the impression that our judge dislikes Guy Gisborne. Unfortunately, she also quizzed your father about his role in your upbringing and she's not your biggest fan.'

'What's she got against me?' Robin asked indignantly.

Ardagh half smiled, then spoke gently. 'Judges are supposed to uphold laws. You have a talent for breaking them.'

'Right,' Robin said awkwardly. 'I hope I don't make you look like a bad parent and ruin your chances.'

Ardagh shook his head and spoke firmly. 'I brought you and your brother up to be decent people. I always gave you freedom to think for yourselves and make your own decisions. I worry about your safety and I can't say I agree with everything you've done, but I am proud of what you've achieved over the last year.'

The court clerk checked his watch as Robin beamed.

'I hate to spoil the party, Mr Hood,' the clerk told Ardagh. 'But you were released into our custody until 21:00 and it will take ten minutes to reach the cells on the far side of the new courthouse.'

'We'll meet properly after you win that appeal,' Robin said, tearing up as he pulled his dad into another hug. 'I'll still be a wanted fugitive, but we'll figure something out.'

'Keep safe,' Ardagh told his son tearfully, as he turned towards the exit. 'I love you.'

'Love you back,' Robin said, then watched from the doorway as Tybalt and his father disappeared down the gloomy corridor.

27. THUNDERBIRD CHICKEN

An hour's nap and the shock of seeing his dad gave Robin a second wind. Central Locksley was dead, so Neo let him ride in the back seat for the short drive to the eastern edge of town.

'How was the bar?' Robin asked.

Neo smiled. 'I got numbers from a couple of girls. Those artsy student types love the idea of having an authentic rebel boyfriend.'

Robin laughed. 'Imagine their parents' reaction if they brought you home.'

'Hah, yes!' Neo laughed, then imitated a young woman's voice. 'Daddy, this is my new boyfriend, Neo. He's wanted in connection with three robberies and last summer he shot holes in a Customs and Immigration speedboat to stop it from capturing thirty migrants . . .'

As Robin kept laughing, Neo spotted the old-skool roadside sign for Thunderbird Chicken.

'You hungry?' Neo asked, though he'd already pulled into the drive-thru lane. 'This joint has been run by the same family for sixty years. Best fried chicken you'll get anywhere.'

Neo then announced that he was broke, so Robin shelled out for a big bucket of chicken, fries and four Cokes. They only got to eat a couple of drumsticks on the move before Neo pulled off-road again and parked behind a burnt-out pet store.

The only other vehicle on the overgrown lot was one of the white vans they'd used to rescue Alan earlier. As Robin and Neo left their car, Ísbjörg got out of the driver's side of the van.

'I got Thunderbird Chicken,' Neo said dramatically, as he held the cardboard bucket over his head like a trophy.

Ísbjörg scowled and told Neo, 'I'm vegan.'

Robin was surprised by the gangly figure in forest gear and a bandana getting out of the passenger side.

'Look at my boy!' Robin told Alan proudly. 'Combat trousers and mud on your boots! I thought you were taking a bath and going to bed.'

'That was the plan,' Alan said, with a shrug. 'But Will Scarlock came to see me after you left. He's an amazing person and he made me feel a lot better.'

Robin nodded in agreement. 'Will and Emma are cool. They created the whole rebel movement out of nothing.'

'I told Will that I felt shaken up and was worried about my family. He said the worst thing to do when you feel bad is to sit around doing nothing, letting the same thoughts churn over and over in your brain . . . Wait, is that Thunderbird Chicken?'

Alan continued his story as he and Robin delved into the bucket of crispy fried chicken.

'Will said getting stuck into the action would make me feel better.'

Robin laughed and spoke with his mouth full. 'Will must like you. He's always trying to *stop* me from getting stuck into the action.'

'Ísbjörg parked near my house on the way here,' Alan continued. 'We couldn't get too close. The place looks pretty wrecked, but Dad's car was on the drive and I saw Dakota moving around in her room.'

'Glad they're OK,' Robin said.

'At least for now,' Alan said warily. 'Then Ísbjörg drove us on to check out Katerina Kendall's home. It's this beat-up double-wide trailer. Looks like a stiff breeze would knock it down.'

'You'd think one of Gisborne's top people would live somewhere better,' Robin noted.

Neo laughed. 'I bet Kendall lives there so she can give herself a nice fat payoff when Gisborne Waste Management wants to buy that area for its next landfill site.'

Ísbjörg seemed irritated by the three males stuffing their faces with fries and chicken as she took over Alan's explanation. 'I took some photographs around Kendall's house. There's a burglar alarm and a couple of mean-looking dogs, and I did a radio frequency sweep. We're right not to get close, because Gisborne definitely has the place bugged.'

'I guess he bugs the homes of all his top people,' Neo said.

Robin nodded. 'You don't stay at the top of an organised crime empire for as long as Gisborne has without being paranoid.'

'Wipe your greasy fingers!' Ísbjörg growled, as Robin reached towards her phone to check out the photos.

'Do have a moist towelette,' Neo said in a silly fake-polite voice, giving Robin a foil-wrapped wipe from the bottom of the chicken bucket.

Once Robin had wiped his hands, he swiped through Ísbjörg's pictures, the other three standing behind him. The house next to the Kendalls' was abandoned, with the roof caved in and a rusted motorhome standing on concrete blocks.

'That motorhome looks perfect,' Robin said. 'We can set the laser microphones up to point at all the windows, and it's flat ground so there won't be any dangerous climbing involved.'

'I read the instructions you forwarded,' Ísbjörg told Robin. 'I've rigged a mobile phone to transmit the audio from the bug, and Unai helped me to wire up a big power pack using lithium cells we stole from TwoTu trucks. If we keep up the surveillance for longer than ten days, someone will have to sneak back and replace the batteries.'

'Is the Kendall place walking distance from here?' Robin asked.

Ísbjörg nodded and pointed at some overgrown land at the back of the lot. 'Three hundred metres. Alan knows the way, so he'll go with you. Neo and I will get rifles from the van and cover your backs in case any of Gisborne's heavies show up.'

'You should go instead of me,' Robin told Ísbjörg. 'I'm half asleep. You built the power pack with Unai and you've read the instructions for the laser microphones. I'm here for my climbing skills, but there isn't any climbing.'

'Maybe Robin and Ísbjörg can go,' Alan suggested.

'You *have* to go,' Robin told Alan. 'You told me you see Heirani's burned face in your nightmares. You can't bring her back to life, but it's just like Will told you: you'll feel a hundred times better when you start fighting back.'

FOUR WEEKS LATER

28. CHICKEN TIME

Robin wiped a gluey eye on the corner of his duvet, then groaned as he rolled and saw 05:57 on his bedside clock. His body begged him to pull up the warm covers and sleep some more, but he swung his legs out and slapped his cheek to wake up.

'Only bloody Tuesday,' Robin groaned to himself.

The underfloor heating didn't come on until six, so the marble was like ice under Robin's feet. He yelped as one of Finn's Lego bricks dug into his heel.

'Keep it down, mate,' Alan teased from his mattress on the floor. 'You know I don't have to get out from under this toasty duvet for two whole delicious hours.'

'Get stuffed,' Robin grunted.

He launched a barefoot kick at Alan's mound of bedding, but not hard enough to do damage. After peeing and dressing in some of the least dirty clothes balled up on the floor, Robin sauntered down the hall towards the kitchen.

Otto always woke up super early, so it was normal to see him in the living room watching cartoons on a tablet, but Robin was surprised to see Indio with Zack in the kitchen. The baby sat in his high chair with a miserable red face and sweaty hair.

'Morning,' Robin said sleepily. 'Something up with the little guy?'

'He's got a slight temperature and he kept waking up with a blocked nose,' Indio explained. 'I guess it's the bug you boys brought back from School Zone.'

'Poor little monster,' Robin said, as he gave Zach a smile.

'I mixed pancake batter,' Indio said, as she stood up and stepped towards the hob. 'If you've got time.'

Robin smiled keenly. 'There's always time for pancakes.'

He usually picked something random out of the fridge and ate it on the way to the chicken sheds, but hot pancakes made it worth getting yelled at for being late.

'Blueberry or chocolate chip?' Indio asked, as she turned on the heat below a large pan.

'One of each,' Robin said, as he opened the fridge and poured a glass of milk.

Indio sighed as the pan warmed up. 'I spoke to Lucy late last night, after her trip to Pelican Island.'

Robin felt a twinge of awkwardness. 'Lucy finally got on the visitors list?' he asked. 'Was Marion OK?'

'As good as can be expected,' Indio said, as three blobs of pancake batter spread across the big pan. 'Most juvenile inmates are sixteen or seventeen, so Marion's one of the smallest. But they've moved her away from the girls who were bullying her. She's now on a different landing, where her cousin Freya Tuck looks out for her.'

'That's a relief,' Robin said.

'She's also seen a surgeon and she's been booked in for the operation she needs on her club foot. And Lucy told her about you clobbering Mr Khan and getting punished.'

Robin half smiled. 'What did Marion say?'

'Apparently she laughed and said *some things never change.*'

Robin fake coughed. 'I've been a model citizen for weeks. I've been to school every day. I've done my chores and every homework on time.'

'Don't expect us to pin a medal on you.' Indio laughed as she turned the pancakes over. 'Kids are *supposed* to go to school and do their homework.'

Robin smiled as he picked up a plastic doll that Zack had knocked off his high chair. It felt like things were getting close to normal with Indio and Karma. They still partly blamed him for Marion getting busted, but you don't make pancakes at six in the morning for someone you can't forgive.

The hot breakfast was an unexpected treat, but added several minutes to Robin's morning routine. He risked taking the unreliable lift down to the ground floor and ran the whole way to the chicken sheds behind the castle.

Robin entered cautiously. He could handle the heat and eye-watering ammonia smell from a thousand pooping birds, but he also expected Chicken Sheila to yell at him for being seven minutes late.

But there was just the noise of hungry chickens – and Josie, with her hair tied back. She wore a blue zip-up overall and rubber boots crusted with chicken manure.

'Afternoon,' Josie said cheekily, as Robin dropped his bow and backpack and started swapping his trainers for manure-spattered wellies. 'Nice of you to drop by . . .'

'Where's Sheila?' Robin asked, as he glanced across at the caged zebras in the adjoining shed.

'I got a message from one of the nurses in the clinic,' Josie explained. 'They took Sheila in last night after she collapsed walking up the stairs to her room. They put her on a drip and kept her in overnight.'

'Sheila won't admit it, but something's really wrong,' Robin said, as he gave Josie a quick peck on the cheek. 'She's lost weight since we moved to the castle, and there wasn't much meat on her beforehand.'

'Blueberry breath and a purple tongue,' Josie noted, before giving Robin a longer kiss on the mouth. 'What girl could resist you?'

'Indio made pancakes.'

'I'll go visit Sheila when we finish feeding and collecting the eggs.'

'She'll yell at you,' Robin warned, as Josie used her pocket knife to slash open a sack of chicken feed.

'No doubt,' Josie said, smiling and shrugging. 'But I'm fond of the old battle-axe, and she'll want to know how many eggs we got.'

As Robin started checking the incubator drawers for newly hatched chicks, Josie stepped into the giant chicken enclosure and began pouring pellets into feed troughs. While the birds went mental fighting over breakfast, Robin cracked a big yawn, then joined Josie in the enclosure to gather eggs that had been laid overnight.

'Did your man in Vietnam send over our Shakespeare homework?' Josie asked.

'He sure did,' Robin said, as he crouched over a scrawny bird that hadn't gone for food and was bloody from being pecked. 'I'll have to put this lady in a separate cage till she heals up.'

'I've got another customer for Year Ten Maths homework,' Josie said.

Robin tutted. 'I wish you wouldn't tell other people about our scam. The more people who know we're paying a dude to do our homework, the more chance we'll get busted, or blackmailed by some smartass like Matt Maid.'

'All right for you to say, Mr Moneybags.' Josie snorted. 'You've got thousands in savings. But selling Maths homework for five quid a pop makes a big difference to my finances.'

'When you get caught, keep my name out of it,' Robin said, as he brushed sawdust and manure off the injured bird, before gently lowering it into a plastic storage box.

'If I stay out of trouble until Friday, I don't have to clean up after school. That means I can switch back to feeding the chickens at night and I don't have to get up at six o'clock seven days a week.'

'I'm only selling homework to people I trust,' Josie said. 'You're being paranoid.'

Robin didn't feel as confident as his girlfriend, but his phone started ringing before he got the chance to answer back.

29. CELEBRITY MASH-UP

Before touching his phone, Robin peeled off his rubber gloves, smeared with poop, sawdust and the injured bird's blood.

'Oluchi, wassup,' Robin said, answering a millisecond before the call went to voicemail. 'Give me a tick, I'm in the chicken shed and it's deafening.'

'I'm up in the Nest,' Oluchi answered. 'I spoke to an old friend, Henry Davenport, last night. He was on my journalism course at uni, and one of the other interns when I worked with Lynn Hoapili at Channel Fourteen. I think he's found an angle that could make this landfill site story exciting enough to make people give a damn.'

'You're spending more time in the Nest than me,' Robin noted, as he exited the chicken enclosure and stepped under an archway into the quieter shed next door, with four bored-looking zebras watching him.

'There's nothing calling me back to the legit world,' Oluchi explained. 'Unless you count student debt, a court summons for unpaid rent, and a crazy mother who wants me to find a handsome Yoruba boy and make lots of babies.'

'So, what have you got that's worth calling me at half six in the morning for?'

'I've listened to everything Katerina Kendall has said in her home office since we planted those microphones a few weeks back. And D'Angela helped me use the information from Nick Adale's laptop to hack into Gisborne Waste Management's entire computer system.

'It's clear that all kinds of illegal waste are being dumped at Gisborne's landfill sites, and I've heard a lot of discussion about cheap ways to fix the gas leaks at Mile End Landfill. But Gisborne is really careful. He keeps phone conversations short and never puts anything in writing. So, if we run the story Gisborne can apologise, sack a few of his senior managers and maybe pay a fine for breaking environmental regulations. It won't do his election campaign any good, but it won't wreck his chance of winning either.'

'What about Heirani and the other two dead workers?' Robin asked.

Oluchi sighed. 'We can prove they're missing, but without bodies I still have no evidence to prove that anyone got murdered. Gisborne could deny everything and suggest that they're hiding in the forest.'

Robin knew that Josie would be annoyed that he wasn't doing his share of the work, so he sounded a touch impatient. 'I don't mean to be rude, Oluchi, but I'm super busy. What's your big breakthrough?'

'One hundred and twenty thousand litres of expired emulsion paint,' Oluchi answered cryptically. 'Paint is highly toxic. None of Gisborne's waste facilities have a licence for processing and disposing of leftover paint, but yesterday I recorded Katerina Kendall on the phone, saying that two tankerloads of paint will be delivered to Gisborne's South Range landfill site late tomorrow afternoon.'

'Interesting,' Robin said. 'But won't Gisborne deny knowing about the paint too?'

'He can't wriggle out of this one,' Oluchi said. 'I have a recording of a phone conversation between Kendall and Gisborne. Gisborne asks her to sort out the paint disposal problem as a favour to Sir Stanley Launcelot.'

'I've heard that name somewhere,' Robin said.

'Launcelot's a businessman who made a fortune with the Sir Savalot DIY stores. He's also a big political donor with lots of friends in senior government positions.'

'Now I get it,' Robin said sharply. 'Sir Stanley has tons of unsold paint to dispose of from his DIY stores. Gisborne is doing him a favour and disposing of his surplus paint because he'll need to make powerful friends in Capital City once he's elected as the new Sheriff of Nottingham.'

'Exactly,' Oluchi said. 'And this is where Darrell Snubs comes in.'

'Snubs?' Robin said, sounding puzzled. 'The stand-up comedian with the long hair, who swears a *lot?*'

'My friend Henry Davenport landed a job as a production assistant on Darrell Snubs' new TV show,' Oluchi explained.

'I watched Snubs' stand-up special with Marion one time,' Robin said. 'She kept going on about how tall and good-looking he was.'

'I wouldn't kick Snubs out of bed,' Oluchi agreed. 'His comedy has got more political in the last few years, and he's done TV debates with politicians where he's discussed you and defended the Sherwood Forest rebels. Henry says Snubs would love to meet you.'

'Seriously?' Robin said, flattered and cracking a big smile. 'That's cool, but what does it have to do with two truckloads of paint?'

'Snubs just launched a new TV series called *Truth to Power*. He goes undercover with anti-hunting groups, environmentalists and anti-poverty campaigners and tries to shame the bad guys.'

'And now he wants to do us?' Robin said.

'Snubs is keen to work with us, but we have to move fast,' Oluchi explained. 'The two tankerloads of paint are being delivered to the South Range landfill site tomorrow afternoon. I only found all this stuff out yesterday, and Darrell Snubs and his producer would like to talk with you this morning to discuss what we can do about it.'

'I've got school,' Robin said warily. 'I know that sounds lame, but I signed a behaviour contract. I'm almost done with my punishments and my life might actually be bearable once I get Will, Emma, Karma, Indio and Mr Khan off my back.'

'Robin, this only works if you're involved,' Oluchi said pleadingly. 'Darrell Snubs teaming up with Robin Hood to fight for justice could turn a story about two truckloads of paint getting dumped into front-page news.'

'Well, I'm always up for a bit of action,' Robin said thoughtfully. 'The behaviour contract does say I can get time off school in *exceptional* circumstances. But Mr Khan gets to decide what counts as exceptional, and he's not exactly my biggest fan . . .'

30. TURN ME UPSIDE DOWN

After three tedious hours being educated about Industrial Era canal building, false perspective and number bases, Robin shot out of his chair on the B of the lunchtime bell.

'Calm down!' his Maths teacher yelled.

Robin barely heard as he charged the door, with Josie steps behind. His stomach growled as he caught delicious smells from the busy food stalls in the resort's atrium, but he kept running. He went under the sign that pointed to the casino, then charged up the dead escalator and sprinted flat out between the rows of slot machines towards the Nest.

'I can't believe we're gonna talk to Darrell Snubs,' Josie gushed as she struggled to match Robin's speed. 'The actual Darrell Snubs!'

Robin smirked as he glanced back. '*I'm* talking to Darrell Snubs. Who even invited you?'

'I've crushed on Snubs since I saw him in a shower gel commercial when I was eight,' Josie said. 'So, either I have an invite, or you have an ex-girlfriend.'

'I just don't see what's so amazing about him,' Robin gasped, slowing down as he reached the door of the Nest, then hit the stairs.

'We got here as fast as we could,' Josie told Oluchi, as she tripped on the top step and nearly sprawled out.

'No worries,' Oluchi said. 'My contact, Henry, called. Darrell Snubs has been running behind schedule all morning, so you're fine.'

But Robin didn't feel fine. As he stepped deeper into the Nest, his nose caught a distinctive smell. It was a mix of cigars, beer, petrol and not washing, and it belonged to two members of the Brigands Motorcycle Club.

The first biker was Luke, one of the gang's newest recruits. Just out of his teens, he had a wispy beard and was spinning around in an office chair like a five-year-old. The second was the monolithically vast figure of gang leader Jake 'Cut-Throat' Maid.

Robin's life flashed in front of his eyes as Cut-Throat stepped close. Especially the bit where he'd encouraged Cut-Throat's daughter, Marion, to take part in a robbery, which led to her getting caught and thrown in jail . . .

'How's life, short stuff?' Cut-Throat bellowed, eyeballing Robin.

Robin's eyes were level with Cut-Throat's belly. Besides his terror, Robin was fascinated by the extraordinary layering of stains on the big man's leather waistcoat.

'I . . .' Robin stuttered, taking half a wobbly step back.

'You look like you're gonna crap your pants,' Cut-Throat said cheerfully. 'What have you got to say for yourself?'

'I'm . . .' Robin began.

He almost said *I'm sorry about Marion*, but decided Cut-Throat wouldn't appreciate weakness.

'I'm not sure if you're angry about what happened to Marion,' Robin spat boldly as he took a nervous glance towards the stairs. 'If you are, can I zip back to the penthouse and grab my bow and arrows?'

Oluchi, Luke and Josie gawped at Robin's cheek, but after a frightening pause Cut-Throat erupted with booming laughter, then lifted Robin effortlessly into the air and flipped him upside down.

'You've got some balls, Robin Hood!' Cut-Throat roared, rattling Robin like a snow globe in one hand, while stretching the other leather-gloved mitt out to shake hands with Josie. 'I could never get Marion to do what she was told, so I know you didn't force that girl into anything.'

Cut-Throat kept up the booming laughter as he dumped a relieved Robin in an office chair, head on the seat cushion and trainers flailing in the air. As Robin clumsily righted himself, he turned towards Oluchi with a furious expression and mouthed, 'You could have warned me.'

Then he looked at Josie, who was wetting herself laughing.

'That was so good.' Josie beamed as Robin picked up all the stuff that had dropped out of his pockets. 'I don't think I've ever seen anyone look *so* scared.'

'I may have aged a couple of years,' Robin admitted, then turned to Cut-Throat. 'If you're not here to kill me, why are you here?'

'She's after Gisborne,' Cut-Throat said, pointing at Oluchi. 'And Gisborne's had it in for us Brigands since we stole thirty cars and blew up Gisborne Prestige Autos last summer.

'Locksley police have been harassing bikers every chance they get, biker bars have been shut down, anyone we try to do business with in the motor trade gets arrested on charges of trading in stolen parts. And if that leather-clad sadist becomes sheriff, our lives won't get any easier.'

Oluchi continued the explanation. 'I've been working on a plan with Darrell Snubs' people. But we'll need muscle to intercept two tanker trucks and their drivers.'

'My Brigands offer plenty of muscle,' Cut-Throat said proudly then looked at Luke, who was still twirling in the office chair. 'Brains not so much . . .'

Robin saw a different angle and added, 'And I suppose you get to keep the two trucks to chop up and sell for parts?'

'That might happen.' Cut-Throat laughed.

A green box on Oluchi's computer started flashing, and Josie gasped as Darrell Snubs appeared on screen.

'It's really him,' Josie squeaked to Robin as Snubs smiled, showing two lines of perfect white teeth.

The comedian's long wavy hair was scruffier than in his online videos, but he still wore a lavishly embroidered waistcoat over a tattooed chest and had masses of chunky gold chains around his neck.

'Greetings, Forest People!' Snubs said theatrically, as everyone in the Nest gathered around Oluchi's screen. 'Robin Hood, it is truly amazing to make your acquaintance.'

'I've watched your comedy specials,' Robin said as he pointed at Josie. 'Though I'm a little jealous because my girlfriend has the hots for you.'

As Snubs laughed, Josie booted Robin in the ankle and turned bright red.

'I'll murder you,' Josie hissed to Robin, as Oluchi told Snubs who everyone was. At the same time her friend Henry joined Snubs on screen.

'I checked the plan you worked out with my boy Henry,' Snubs said. 'I reckon this is gonna make an amazing episode of my new series, and show voters in Nottinghamshire what a weaselly murdering dirtbag Guy Gisborne is.'

'Our publicity department did some market research,' Henry added excitedly. 'When we asked viewers aged 13 to 49 what they thought about Darrell Snubs and Robin

Hood teaming up, over eighty-six per cent said it was something they'd like to watch.'

'It'll be must-see TV if we pull off Oluchi's plan,' Snubs added, as he got out of his chair and gave a little wave. 'Now I've got to dash off for a very important hair appointment. But you can sort all the details with Henry and I'll meet y'all in the flesh tomorrow.'

Barely a minute after logging on, Darrell Snubs dashed away from the webcam and left things to his young production assistant.

'Darrell's an extremely busy man,' Henry said apologetically, as he moved his webcam so he was in the middle of the screen.

Cut-Throat leaned in towards Oluchi's screen and sounded furious. 'That's disrespectful,' he growled. 'I stood here for half an hour waiting to talk to Snubs, and he ditches to visit his hairdresser? If that was a face-to-face meeting, it wouldn't be his hair getting cut off . . .'

Henry looked worried. Oluchi had been researching and trying to build a story about Gisborne for almost a month and was keen to keep things on track.

'Darrell Snubs is a figurehead,' she told Cut-Throat warily. 'It doesn't matter if he's a bit of a dick. What matters is that Snubs has thirty million followers on social media and seven million who watch his TV show. He can make this story big enough to stop Guy Gisborne being elected as sheriff.'

Henry ran a nervous hand through his curly red hair and nodded in agreement. 'Let's go carefully through the plan for the whole operation.'

'I don't do details,' Cut-Throat told Oluchi as he waved his hand dismissively. 'I'm going to the atrium to get lunch. Tell me what you need and when you need it, but you warn Darrell Snubs and his fancy hairdo to stay out of my way.'

As the two Brigands stormed out of the Nest, Cut-Throat looked back at Robin and Josie. 'Aren't you kids on lunch break? Come with me. I'll make Luke buy you cheeseburgers.'

31. EXCEPTIONAL CIRCUMSTANCES

The worst part of cleaning up after school was the boys' toilets. The little lads couldn't aim straight, and once Matt Maid and his gang realised Robin was cleaning up after them, they decided it was hilarious to smear soap on the mirrors and block sinks with clumps of soggy toilet paper.

Everything sparkled when Robin mopped his way out of the toilets. He emptied grey water from the mop bucket into a sink in the cleaner's store room, peeled off his rubber gloves, and imagined giving Matt Maid a good kick up the arse as he lathered his hands with antibacterial soap.

Once he'd towelled off, Robin locked the store room, dropped two rubbish bags down a trash chute, then knocked on Mr Khan's office door.

'Enter,' Mr Khan said, stiff and pompous as always.

'I'm done,' Robin said tiredly, as he walked in and put the store room key on Mr Khan's desk.

Khan peered over the top of his reading glasses. 'Did you scrub the paint pots in the art room like Mrs Schreiber asked?'

'Yes, sir.'

'And you wiped the sink down afterwards?'

'Of course.' Robin grunted. 'Like every other time I've done it.'

Khan didn't appreciate Robin's surly tone. '*Both* dishwashers in the kitchen?'

'Just like you asked,' Robin said. 'Plates and cutlery stacked up ready for the forest kids' breakfast club.'

Khan paused, like he was trying to think of something else, then snorted. 'Well, I guess you can go up to your fancy penthouse and get on with your homework.'

Robin twitched nervously. 'I need to ask if I can take tomorrow afternoon off.'

Kahn rolled his chair back and both eyebrows shot up in outrage.

'Who died?' Khan asked.

'Nobody died,' Robin said, too anxious to realise that Khan was making a joke.

'So, what is the exceptional circumstance?'

Robin gave a brief explanation, about Oluchi's investigation into the three deaths at Mile End Landfill and how they were going to team up with Darrell Snubs and the Brigands to intercept the paint trucks and ruin Guy Gisborne's attempt to be the new sheriff.

'Sounds overly complicated,' Khan said.

Robin looked confused. 'I've done everything you've asked me to, sir. I'll make up any work I miss tomorrow over the weekend.'

'Not you, Hood,' Khan said. 'I'm talking about the plan you just described. Why get Brigands to intercept trucks in a hostile situation?'

'You have to stop trucks somehow.'

'Forest Rangers,' Khan said cryptically, as he locked his fingers together and gave Robin a sly smile. 'They're supposed to police all of Sherwood Forest, but they're understaffed and underfunded so they just patrol a few major forest roads. I worked with rangers and made friends back when I was a cop. They're no fans of Gisborne, and I'm sure they'll let me borrow a couple of Ranger trucks and a few sets of uniform.'

Robin knew Mr Khan responded to flattery. 'That *does* sound like a better idea, sir. Vehicles near the forest get stopped at Forest Ranger roadblocks all the time. It'll be way easier than having a bunch of bikers try to force the trucks off the road.'

'I've not spoken to your friend Oluchi, but she's quite young, isn't she?'

'Twenty-two, I think,' Robin said, as Mr Khan stood up.

'I'm guessing she doesn't have experience planning a tactical operation,' Khan said. 'She will benefit from my expertise.'

This wasn't what Robin expected, and he wasn't sure how Oluchi would respond to Mr Khan's offer of help.

'I was only asking for the afternoon off,' Robin said.

Khan tutted and looked at Robin like he was an idiot. 'The operation you described can't work without the publicity generated by you and Darrell Snubs. I think you should take the whole day off school so you're properly rested. Now where is Oluchi? In that den-nest thingy of yours? I'll speak with her right away.'

Mr Khan took his blazer down from a hook and his keys from the desktop.

'No time to waste!' he said enthusiastically. 'Don't dilly-dally!'

As Mr Khan locked the main School Zone corridor, Robin was surprised to see bikers Luke and Cut-Throat slouched in leather armchairs in the adjoining lounge.

'Are things going to plan?' Cut-Throat asked Robin, the giant standing up and eyeing Khan suspiciously.

'I guess,' Robin said. 'What brings you guys down here?'

'Oluchi's plan doesn't work without you,' Cut-Throat told Robin, as he ground his giant fist into his palm. 'If your headmaster said no, I thought I could use my persuasive powers on him.'

Mr Khan heard this and looked furious.

Robin looked pleadingly at Khan. 'I did not know these guys were out here, I swear.'

Cut-Throat stepped closer to Khan and wagged his index finger. 'I know you,' he growled menacingly.

Khan was as tall as Cut-Throat, but weighed half as much. However, the cop-turned-headmaster had faced off plenty of tough guys and refused to look intimidated. 'I've seen you around the castle, Mr Maid, and at the outlet mall before it got burned.'

'I knew you long before that,' Cut-Throat said, as he went eyeball to eyeball with Khan. 'I recall blasting my first Harley motorcycle down Locksley High Street. A wiry young cop pulled me over. Said I was speeding. Found out that I had no insurance. I offered him all the cash I had on me as a bribe, but he wouldn't take it. The sheriff's office confiscated my bike and locked me up for seven days.'

'I've never taken a bribe in my life,' Khan told Cut-Throat determinedly. 'Not from you. Not when Gisborne's thugs threatened my family.'

Robin wasn't sure if Khan and Cut-Throat were going to hug it out or start trading punches. Luckily it was the former.

Cut-Throat cracked a slight smile. 'Just my rotten luck, getting stopped by the last honest cop in Locksley.'

Khan smiled slightly too. 'It's thirty years since I was a newbie officer on traffic patrol.'

'Before me and Luke were born,' Robin said, trying to keep the mood light. 'Bet you guys never could have imagined that you'd end up working on the same side.'

'I did not,' Khan said cheerfully, as Cut-Throat nodded in agreement. 'Shall we find young Oluchi and get this plan of hers knocked into shape?'

'Gisborne threatened your family?' Cut-Throat said as he gave Khan a friendly thump on the shoulder. 'I guess that gives you at least as much reason to hate him as I do.'

32. OLYMPIC STYLE

The operation kicked off at two the following afternoon. Robin was buzzing. After thirty dreary days hosing chicken sheds, squirting bleach down toilets and cheating his way through vast quantities of homework, he'd been let off the leash to do something exciting.

Not only was the plan complicated, but every step had to be filmed for the upcoming episode of *Truth to Power*.

Robin sat in the rear compartment of an unmarked TV production van surrounded by racks of lights, cameras and editing gear. An assistant named Larry stooped over him, dabbing on make-up with a cotton pad.

'It's a light foundation,' Larry explained, as a camera team setting up equipment outside sent a large tripod clattering against the side of the van. 'It stops your skin from reflecting light and looking greasy. Now lift your hair off your forehead for me and . . .'

Robin felt a tickle as he pulled back his hair to let Larry dust his forehead with powder.

'I'll need to touch that up once in a while,' Larry said, as he pulled a tiny action camera out of a case and used a spring clip to attach it to the pocket of Robin's plaid shirt. 'I'm going to set this camera to record and it will keep running for ten hours. The footage might be shaky, but hopefully we'll get some cool shots of you running and jumping off stuff. And the microphone is on the whole time, so don't say anything rude about me, OK?'

Robin grinned and looked down at the camera. 'What if I need to use the toilet or something?'

'Press the red pause button,' Larry said, as he held up a little hand mirror so Robin could see how he looked. 'But don't forget to restart the recording afterwards.'

'Nice job hiding the zits on my neck,' Robin noted.

'My pleasure,' Larry said, as he opened the van's sliding side door. 'You're free to go, but try not to rub your face.'

Robin jumped out the back of the van into the wintry parking lot. It was beside Route 24, fifty kilometres south of Sherwood Forest.

There were tripods and equipment bags leaning against the van. As one guy set up a drone and a two-person camera crew checked lights and focus, Oluchi stood alone in a fat red puffa jacket, practising a speech she was about to give to camera:

'I'm standing in a truck stop, awaiting the arrival of two tankers containing enough toxic paint sludge to fill an Olympic-style swimming pool . . . Dammit, that's wrong . . . An Olympic-*sized* swimming pool.

'If our sources are correct, the drivers will stop here to use the facilities and eat lunch. While they do that, one special guest member of the *Truth to Power* team will fit tracking devices to the trucks so we can see where they go. You might have heard of him before. His name is Robin Hood.'

'Nice intro,' Robin said, trying to sooth Oluchi's nerves.

Oluchi didn't share his confidence. 'Henry Davenport says if I nail this gig, there's a real chance I'll be brought on board as a presenter-slash-researcher for the rest of the series. It could be my big break. But only if I can stop saying *Olympic-style swimming pool . . .*'

'You'll soon be more famous than your old boss Lynn Hoapili,' Robin joked, as his eyes were drawn to the biker Luke, wheeling a powerful Kawasaki dirt bike down a ramp at the back of another parked van.

Oluchi laughed. 'More famous than Robin Hood?'

'Nobody's that famous,' Robin joked. 'I've gotta go check out my new dirt bike.'

But as Robin headed over to Luke, one of the runners for Snubs' TV show came bowling over the grassy mound that separated the lot they were parked in from an adjoining truck stop.

'Tankers just arrived!' she gasped. 'We got some sneaky footage of them driving in, but we need to move fast in case the drivers don't stop to eat.'

Robin suddenly had three TV people around him, one checking his shirt-pocket camera, one fitting an earpiece radio, and the third handing him the two magnetic tracking devices and asking if he knew what to do with them.

'Stick 'em to the truck,' Robin answered. 'Have you turned them on?'

'What? Wait. No, I haven't actually switched them on . . .'

As Robin rolled his eyes, Larry the make-up guy gave him a last-second touch-up and Oluchi panicked because she still hadn't filmed her intro.

'It's not live, Oluchi,' Paul the director told her patronisingly. 'We can film the intro and Robin driving off on the dirt bike *afterwards*.'

The TV people didn't seem too organised, so Robin satisfied himself that his lapel camera and the tracking devices were working before looking behind at Daisy, the absurdly energetic young camera operator tasked with trailing him. She'd be using a handheld camera no bigger than a smartphone, because anything bigger would attract attention.

'Robin, ready?' the director asked. 'Camera, ready?'

Robin held one tracking device in each hand as he set off at a brisk walk, Daisy a few steps behind.

'Can you run?' Daisy asked. 'It looks more dramatic.'

'But also more suspicious,' Robin said, sticking determinedly to walking pace.

At the top of the little grass embankment, Robin got a view over a busy truck stop with close to a hundred parked vehicles. On the far side, truckers who'd already hit their daily ten-hour driving limit were parked up, ready to spend the night sleeping in their cabs. In the centre, drivers smoked and gossiped outside a busy café that adjoined showers, toilets and a huge refuelling station.

There were close to a dozen tankers parked up, but while most were crisply painted with the logos of major oil and chemical companies, Robin's targets were rust-streaked hulks, years past their prime.

As Robin got to the back of the tanker, he spotted a metal safety warning plate with a Sir Savalot logo at the top.

'Film that,' Robin told Daisy. 'Proves who owns the tanker.'

As they cut between the two parked tankers, a passing driver spotted them and stopped walking. He looked suspicious because you don't see many women and kids in truck stops, but fortunately he chose not to stick his nose in and moved on.

Robin reached behind the rearmost tyre of one truck. The magnetic tracker pulled itself up to the underside of the wheel arch and hit with a satisfying clank. Daisy moved in with the smartphone to get a close-up shot as Robin did the same with the other tanker.

'Now, look back over your shoulder and say something dramatic,' Daisy urged.

Robin tutted. 'That guy who stopped might warn someone. We need to get out of here.'

Daisy said nothing, but kept the camera pointing in Robin's face.

'OK, fine.' Robin groaned, then tried to sound like he was narrating an advert for an extremely powerful toilet cleaner. 'And now, the tracking devices are in place and the first stage of our plan is complete. Let's see where our toxic cargo is heading.'

33. IT'S ALL FAKE ON TV

The two tankers left the truck stop, Oluchi stood on the grass mound to record her intro, then Paul the director and three camera operators spent ten minutes filming close-ups of Robin. These would be edited together to make a cool sequence of Robin removing sunglasses, then putting on a leather biker jacket, gloves and helmet, before straddling the bright yellow dirt bike and blasting off into the late afternoon sun.

The director had planned out a dramatic storyline, with shots of Robin tracking the tankers on his bike intercut with a 3D map showing their progress, while Darrel Snubs would add a lively voiceover.

All this would look cool on the telly, but realistically a kid riding a bright yellow dirt bike along the busy eight-lane Route 24 would result in dozens of concerned motorists calling the cops. And there was no need to follow the tankers closely because the signal from the tracking devices could be picked up from ten kilometres away.

Once the director had enough fake footage, Robin helped Luke roll the two dirt bikes back into the van, then took a less glamorous ride in the middle seat of the production van. Oluchi sat in the other passenger seat, while make-up guy Larry drove.

For safety reasons, the law restricted heavy chemical-filled tankers to eighty kilometres per hour, and there were weight limits on many of Locksley's dilapidated bridges. While the two tankers lumbered along main roads, the convoy of three TV vans and two seven-seat people carriers overtook the tankers on Route 24 and shaved twenty minutes off their journey time by cutting through housing estates and country roads.

The South Range landfill site was north of Locksley, less than a kilometre from Sherwood Forest. The name came from the land's original use as an army firing range, and as the convoy of TV people skimmed past its buckled, rusted perimeter fence, Robin saw aged yellow signs with pictures of tanks and *DANGER: UNEXPLODED SHELLS* written underneath.

'I wonder if anyone got blown up when they dug the hole to make a landfill?' Robin asked.

He didn't expect an answer, but got one from Oluchi in the passenger seat. 'I actually looked into that. The government spent millions clearing up all the unexploded ordnance. Then Gisborne bought the land for a fraction of what it was worth.'

Robin snorted. 'I bet some corrupt general retired to the Caribbean with a few suitcases stuffed with Gisborne's cash.'

Unlike Mile End Landfill, with its kilometres of neat fencing and uniformed staff coordinating the lines of carts dumping trash, South Range was a much older facility with a shabby vibe and just a pair of maintenance trucks parked in the concourse behind the main gate.

'At least it doesn't stink like Mile End,' Oluchi noted. 'This site is officially retired. All the dumps are capped with soil and they're only licensed to bring in waste to deal with settlement.'

'Settlement?' Robin asked curiously. 'Like if trash rots down and a hole opens up?'

'Exactly,' Oluchi agreed. 'But I got the Super to dig up satellite images from the last month, and there are still trucks and tankers stopping here every day. It's less than what gets dumped at Mile End in ten minutes, but if you want to ditch something toxic or illegal, they do it here where there aren't hundreds of potential witnesses.'

Larry the make-up guy led the five-vehicle convoy on for another couple of kilometres, then steered tentatively off-road and down a rutted gravel track with overhanging branches that clattered against the sides of the van.

'How near is Sherwood Forest?' Larry asked nervously, as they passed a trio of burnt-out barns and swampy fields that were no longer farmed due to persistent flooding.

'A couple of hundred metres from the official boundary,' Robin said, amused by Larry's nervousness. 'But don't worry, I'll look after you.'

The crest of a hill brought a sloping grass field and a ragtag gathering into view. There were more TV production vans, similar to the one Robin was riding in, two four-wheel drives that were too clean to belong to anyone who lived out here, three bright orange Forest Ranger trucks and, absurdly, a metallic silver truck, its long trailer fitted with air-conditioning units and blacked-out windows.

Robin's boots splattered mud up his trousers as he jumped out of the van behind Oluchi, then squelched as he swung around to grab his backpack and bow from the cargo compartment. He was amused to see Mr Khan and a few other rebels wearing Forest Ranger uniform, while bored-looking Brigands with rifles stood around the edge of the field for security.

As Robin overheard one of the TV people tell Oluchi that the tankers were still twenty minutes away, he was approached by a tall woman with a large tablet PC. She had a fashion model's spindly limbs and chiselled features, and rattled off words like machine-gun bullets.

'Robin Hood, I'm Mia, personal assistant to Mr Snubs. He has a seven-minute window and he's extremely keen to see you in his trailer before we film the sequence where you meet for the first time and hug it out.'

Robin had thought the TV stuff would be cool, but it was actually super fake and irritating. 'Seven whole minutes,' he said, unable to hide a smirk. 'I'm truly honoured.'

Mia didn't appreciate the sarcasm and slipped as she tried to lift her flowery-patterned boot out of the mud. It took all Robin's strength to grasp Mia's upper arm and stop her falling in the dirt, but instead of a thank you she gave Robin a *how dare you touch me?* scowl.

'I signed up to work for a comedian,' Mia growled to herself as she squelched off towards the big silver trailer with a bemused Robin in tow. 'The only mud in my life should be a face pack in a beauty salon.'

34. A MINOR GLITCH

Robin had never met a big celebrity before and felt awkward as he stood on a tarp in front of the trailer, unlacing his muddy boots.

'Don't sweat over the mud, kid,' Darrell Snubs said, beaming and confident as he kicked open the trailer's big silver door, dressed in tight leather trousers, a leopard-print waistcoat over his bare chest, and his trademark gold chains. 'I have assistants who deal with dirt.'

Robin enjoyed Mia's furious expression as he stomped mud up the steps and into the lavishly appointed trailer. The area by the entrance was a kitchen full of fancy appliances, while a little sausage dog napped in a basket shaped like a giant bone.

Beyond the kitchen was a lounge with recliner chairs and an elaborately lit bar with racks of coloured bottles. At the far end Robin glimpsed, through sliding doors, a room with mirrored walls and a bed covered in fur quilts.

'Nice crib,' Robin observed as he glanced about, although he couldn't help feeling that driving around rural roads in this monstrous silver trailer wasn't the best way to keep things under wraps.

'You've got your famous bow,' Snubs said as he stepped through to the lounge and flopped down in a recliner chair. 'Do take the weight off.'

'Bow never leaves my side,' Robin explained, getting swallowed by a huge puffy armchair while Snubs picked up a remote and turned off a TV playing a thrash metal video. 'Except weapons aren't allowed in school.'

'I was speaking to my director, Paul,' Snubs said. 'I thought it might be fun to shoot a kind of cute buddy sequence with the two of us. You know, where you show me how to use a bow and arrow. Or maybe you could do some archery stunt type thing.'

'I thought this new show was serious,' Robin said, as he noticed the muddy boot prints he'd left across a furry rug. 'Politics, protestors and stuff.'

Snubs leaned forward in his chair and sounded more intense. 'I'm trying to push limits with *Truth to Power*. Serious issues, done in an entertaining way. I want to raise awareness among people who wouldn't read a newspaper or watch old farts interviewed on some politics show.'

'I could do the classic skit and shoot an apple off your head,' Robin suggested. 'It's a super easy shot, but I bet your director could make it look dramatic, with slow motion and stuff.'

'You're a little genius!' Snubs said, clapping his hands and bouncing in his chair like a toddler who needed the toilet. 'It would be amazing for the episode trailer, or we could do it as a standalone bit to push out on my social media channels.

'I can do an intro to camera with an apple on my head. Then the arrow hits in slow motion and the camera swings around to reveal that it was fired by you.'

Snubs looked excitedly at his assistant, who'd just appeared in the lounge doorway. 'Mia, I need you to get Paul in here. We need to set up and shoot an extra sequence with Robin for a trailer.'

Mia shook her head sharply. 'Darrell, you need your boots on and your wireless mic fitted. The tankers are less than ten minutes away and Paul wants you in shot when we film the Forest Ranger trucks heading out to set up the roadblock.'

'Aye, aye, boss lady,' Snubs said, shooting out of the chair and saluting as Mia rushed back to the bedroom to find his boots. 'Robin, I shall be back presently. There's a ton of food in my fridge if you want a bite.'

Robin was hungry. When Snubs and Mia rushed out of the trailer, he opened a fridge stuffed with beers and fancy food platters. He wedged a savoury beef patty in his mouth and grabbed four king prawn skewers. But there was no way he was going to miss the action outside, so he jumped down the trailer's front steps and ate as he crossed the thick mud towards the Forest Ranger trucks.

This part of the plan was simple and didn't involve Robin. The Ranger trucks Mr Khan borrowed would be driven down to the road and used to create a fake roadblock. The tankers would be forced to stop and the drivers would be kicked out and replaced by two rebels, who'd drive the tankers to a safe hiding place and prepare them for the second phase of the plan.

Robin stayed in the background, leaning against one of the TV company's people carriers as the three Forest Ranger trucks prepared to leave. Darrell Snubs and Oluchi stood side by side recording a bit to a camera, and Mr Khan fumed because a twenty-year-old TV production assistant was telling him not to leave until a camera operator was free to film his departure.

'There isn't time,' Khan shouted, as he stood by an orange truck in a tan Ranger's uniform in trousers that were way too tight. 'If we don't stop the tankers, this whole plan is a bust.'

Paul the director finally grasped that time was an issue. He told Darrell to run across to the Ranger trucks so they could show him in the thick of the action as they drove away. Amidst the chaos, a runner from the TV crew gave Mia a large video light to carry and Robin cracked up laughing as she overbalanced and went sideways into the mud.

Mr Khan started the engine of the lead truck, but only drove ten metres before there were three loud bangs that shredded his front tyre.

'What was that?' Snubs shouted, as he squatted down on his haunches. 'Is that gunfire?'

Everyone hit the muddy ground as more sharp cracks shot across the field, followed by the dazzling white blast from a pair of stun grenades.

Robin shuddered and took cover in thick mud under a people carrier, but the grenade had dazzled him and all he could see was a blue-white blur. The arrows sticking out of his backpack snagged the underside of the vehicle and his trousers stuck to the wet ground as he tried to work out which direction the attack was coming from.

After a few long blinks Robin started to get some vision back. There was nobody near him, but it was chaos around the Ranger trucks thirty metres away. Fake Rangers and terrified TV people squatted on the ground, while at least eight bandits with guns and body armour charged in to surround them.

'On your knees, hands on head!'

'Money, phones and car keys, or we'll shoot holes in you.'

More bandits, including a trailing pack of grubby forest kids, charged into the field and began looting equipment from TV production vans. When Robin looked the other way, he saw two women with shotguns entering Snubs' silver trailer.

The site perimeter was supposed to have been secured by the Brigands, but they were a disorganised bunch and

Robin wasn't entirely surprised that they'd disappeared into hedges around the field at the first sign of trouble.

None of the bandits seemed to have spotted Robin, but they'd surely try to steal the people carrier he was hiding under. And if they got their hands on Robin, their minds would turn to the half-a-million-pound bounty that Guy Gisborne had put on his head.

35. THE VIEW FROM ABOVE

The nearest cover was a thicket of trees and bushes fifty metres from Robin's position. The blinding grenade flashes meant he still hadn't worked out where the bandits came from, but the risk of staying put seemed greater than the risk of running into the bandits he was trying to get away from.

Nerves, thick mud and the tightness of the space under the car meant Robin took ages to pull three arrows and notch one ready to shoot. Big clumps of dirt slid down his trouser legs as he ran flat out for ten seconds and crashed into thick bushes.

He briefly considered running to the hedge around the field's edge and heading north into the forest. This would guarantee his own safety, but down by the Ranger trucks the bandits were tearing off jewellery and roughing people up.

Mr Khan took a smack to the head as he resisted a guy with a gun demanding the password for his phone.

Oluchi and a bunch of TV people had been ordered to hand over valuables, then got humiliated by being forced to lie face down in a puddle.

Darrell Snubs' celebrity earned him special attention. He'd been stripped of his gold chains and blingy diamond watch, and was now the subject of a lively bandit debate on the merits of taking him hostage.

'I hate bandits,' Robin growled to himself as he began a rapid, expert tree-climb.

There were no leaves to give cover at this time of year, so he stuck close to the trunk. At twelve metres up, he straddled a thick branch and carefully surveyed the field.

The group of bandits debating Snubs' kidnapping had grown bigger and louder. The women who'd entered his trailer were stuffing one of the TV crew's four-wheel drives with designer clothes, jewellery and booze, while a boy no older than eight stumbled over muddy ground carrying three of the TV company's pricy video-editing laptops.

The air of chaos made Robin confident that the bandit attack was an unplanned encounter. He thought it might be safest to stay hidden in the tree until the bandits stole all they could carry and vanished back into the forest. But the four Brigand guards who'd initially retreated had their own plan.

From his vantage point, Robin was first to see the bearded Brigands marching in a line. Three fired shotguns over the heads of the group around Darrell Snubs, while the fourth closed in on a truck and blasted a rifle round through its radiator as some bandits tried to drive it away. This was smart, because as well as stopping the truck, it blocked the single-lane track that was the only way a vehicle could leave the boggy field.

While the Brigands reloaded their weapons and took cover, most adult bandits and all of the kids scattered towards the hedges or into the forest with whatever they could carry. But a determined group remained close to Darrell and the Forest Ranger trucks.

The two female and three male bandits backed away from all their hostages, except Snubs, who got dragged by the biggest bandit as they took defensive positions behind the Ranger trucks. All five wore modern ballistic helmets and bulletproof vests, and held automatic rifles that gave them more firepower than the Brigand guards' shotguns.

As Darrell Snubs tried sitting up and got a brutal boot in the ribs for his trouble, Robin saw a million ways that a standoff between angry Brigands and well-equipped bandits could end in a bloodbath.

His spot in the tree gave him a clear line of sight to the bandits crouching between Ranger trucks and their captives squirming in the mud nearby. He took aim at a beefy female bandit, whose position made her the easiest target.

Her bulletproof vest wasn't a problem, because Robin knew they were designed to absorb the energy from bullets, which break up on impact, not knives or arrows, which penetrate with a sharp point.

For a minute that felt more like ten, the Brigands and hardcore bandits were locked in their uneasy standoff, while TV people shivered in the mud, too scared to move. Eventually, one bandit got so frustrated that he bobbed up over the hood of a Ranger truck and sprayed bullets randomly towards the last place he'd seen Brigands.

This was the distraction Robin needed. While several hostages screamed and one Brigand blasted back, he notched, aimed and fired four arrows in four seconds. The first hit the bandit who'd started shooting in the upper arm. Two speared the body armour of crouching bandits, while the last caught a bandit as he turned to run away, shattering his hip bone.

Robin had given his position away by firing the arrows, and he leaped out of the tree before any bandits could shoot back. As he landed in the mud after a four-metre drop, the emboldened Brigand guards launched another shotgun volley, while Mr Khan acted bravely, charging the bandit Robin had shot in the hip and ripping away his assault rifle.

Robin's fast, accurate shooting had terrified the bandits. They didn't know he'd already left his shooting position and, as the Brigands closed in, they began to scatter. He kept three arrows at the ready as he gave the hobbling bandits time to clear the scene, then he sprinted towards the Forest Ranger trucks.

The captives were shocked and shivering, and a couple vomited as they stood up. They'd lost their phones, money and valuable equipment from the production vans, but so far as Robin could tell there were only two moderate injuries.

The first was a cameraman whose leg had got burned when the stun grenade exploded next to him, while Darrell Snubs had taken a lick from everyone who wanted to be able to say they'd kicked a big-time celebrity, and had a bloody neck where his gold chains had been ripped off.

'It's OK, they've gone,' Robin told Oluchi, when he found her squatting against the side of a trashed production van, soaked, shivering and tearful.

Oluchi wiped away tears with her palm and tipped her head back. Robin opened a backpack and handed her the small towel he used to keep his archery gear dry.

'I put so much work into this,' she sobbed. 'Now the road out is blocked, the tankers will be gone already, and most equipment is stolen or smashed.'

'I know, it sucks,' Robin said soothingly. 'At least nobody was badly hurt.'

The chaotic bandit crew hadn't taken everything, and Daisy the camera operator had already attached a battery pack to a handheld camera and was using it to film the aftermath.

'Someone take a photo of my bloody neck,' Darrell Snubs was demanding. 'Put it online. Tag it, *What just happened to me?* My chains getting robbed will be massive news!'

While Snubs worried about his social media profile, Robin's eye caught the young biker Luke and the four Brigand guards standing nearby. They made him think of motorbikes, which made him think of the two powerful yellow dirt bikes and the fact that he hadn't seen bandits riding them or going inside the truck that was storing them.

Robin ran over to the Ranger trucks near Mr Khan, Darrell Snubs and Paul the director. Then he took a big breath and shouted to everyone.

'We've put a ton of work into this and I don't think we should give up. If we use motorbikes, we might still catch those tankers before they dump all the paint at the landfill site.'

Robin heard some positive noises, but mostly people shook their heads and tutted like they thought he was deluded.

'And then what?' Mr Khan asked. His trousers were ripped and he held an assault rifle.

'I've never done an operation where something hasn't gone wrong,' Robin said determinedly. 'Let's catch those tankers before they dump the paint. We can figure out the rest when we get there.'

36. A ROBIN HOOD PRODUCTION

He was the smallest person in the field, but while some people were in shock, doubled up, crying, hugging, or sucking on their inhalers, Robin's brain had kicked into gear.

As he ran across the field to the truck with the two yellow dirt bikes inside, Robin realised he had no idea how to open the back doors. But as he skidded to a halt, and almost went down in the mud, the young Brigand Luke was right behind.

By the time Luke had the truck doors open, there was another massive Brigand on the scene, pulling out the metal ramp so the bikes could drive away.

'I'll be right behind on my Harley,' the Brigand shouted, running off as fast as his bulk allowed.

Robin's motorbike-riding skills were average at best, and he tried to remember all the stuff Marion had taught him as he walked up the ramp, straddled a bike and gave it a kick-start.

Luke was an expert rider, and set off down the ramp first. Robin let out the throttle and got more power than he'd expected. The ramp made an alarming clanking sound as he shot out of the truck, wobbling, then almost flying over the handlebars when the front wheel bedded in the muddy ground.

'Can you ride that thing?' Luke asked, driving slowly and looking backwards.

'I guess we'll find out,' Robin said.

As Luke led the bikes across the field towards the road, two more Brigands were starting their Harleys. At the bottom of the field, Mr Khan had organised a group of TV people to push back the four-wheel drive blocking the exit road. When Luke slowed down to steer around them, he got flagged down by Daisy the camera operator.

'Can I ride with you?' she asked, then jumped on behind Luke, one hand wrapped around his waist and the other bravely holding a camera.

'We'll catch up in the trucks once we've cleared the path,' Mr Khan shouted as the bike convoy shot past.

Luke sped down the gravel path with three bulky Brigand bikes close behind. Robin tried to stay close, but dropped back when he found himself breathing chalky dust and pelted with stones thrown up by their back wheels.

'Hell, yeah!' Luke said, punching the air exuberantly when they hit the tree-lined road. 'Brigands in the house!'

Robin felt more confident on tarmac and his nimble dirt bike swept past the three Brigands on their big Harley cruisers.

'Let Robin lead,' Daisy urged, her camera balanced precariously on one shoulder. 'I want to film him leading the charge.'

Robin followed orders, but the road wasn't wide and he wobbled when two guys in fancy sports cars sped around the corner in the other direction. Fortunately, the entire trip was only three kilometres. He dropped back and played it safe until they turned onto a short slip road at the dilapidated gates of South Range landfill site.

'Now what?' Luke asked.

As Robin stepped off his bike, he realised Daisy had the camera pointing his way and everyone seemed to expect him to know what to do next. It was starting to get dark, and he could see one of the battered tankers parked on a muddy lot twenty metres beyond the gate.

'Can I help you fellas?' a rough-looking dude asked, walking up to the inside of the gate. He wore the same orange overall as the workers at Mile End Landfill, but it had so many rips you could see more of the hoodie beneath it.

As Robin looked awkwardly at his boots, hoping for a bright idea, a Brigand who everyone called Ratbreath – on account of his black, rotten teeth – approached the fence and tried to talk his way in.

'Hoping we can do some business, mister,' Ratbreath improvised. 'Got a whole bunch of stripped-down car chassis that we need to make disappear. I figure you're running the kind of place that can help with that.'

The Brigands had a nasty reputation, and the man inside the fence raised both hands submissively.

'I see who you are and I don't want to get on the wrong side of you,' the man began. 'But this landfill is Gisborne's property. I know he has a beef with you bikers, and I'll be toast if he finds out that I helped you.'

As Ratbreath smiled and tried to stay cool, Daisy filmed from a discreet distance, while Robin kept out of sight and looked hopefully for a gap in the fence, or a place where he could climb without getting snagged by the massive curls of barbed wire at the top.

'Four thousand cash in your pocket and Gisborne need never know,' Ratbreath said. 'Let me inside, buddy. We'll bash out a deal.'

But the man wasn't buying Ratbreath's story and backed up from the gate.

'I just want to do my job, mate,' he stuttered. 'I've got a tanker emptying a load of paint down the hill and another to do straight after. I mean the Brigands Motorcycle Club no disrespect, but I can't help you out.'

Daisy smiled, because she'd filmed the guy admitting that they were dumping paint. Robin looked back towards the main road because he could hear vehicles coming. Then a voice broke out in his earpiece radio.

'This is Khan. What's happening down there? Over.'

Robin tapped his earpiece to answer back. 'Both tankers inside. One is full, one emptying out already, but we can't get through the gate.'

'I'll come in fast,' Khan answered. 'Get your bodies and bikes out of the way.'

As Khan said this, Robin saw the outlines of two Ranger trucks on the gloomy road and shouted back to the others.

'Clear our gear!'

As Robin wheeled his dirt bike away, the man inside the gate realised what was about to happen and went into full panic, pulling his phone from his hoodie pocket as he turned to run.

'You don't snitch!' Ratbreath shouted after him. 'Drop that phone or we'll come after you!'

37. OPEN SESAME

Daisy squatted close to the gate, shooting with the news camera as the last Harley got wheeled out of the way. Mr Khan swerved off the main road, then blasted the horn as the metal bull bars on the front of the Forest Ranger truck ploughed into the metal and mesh gate.

The front of the orange truck crumpled and six airbags exploded inside. The crash hadn't fully opened the gate, but it had made a gap big enough for Luke, Ratbreath and the other two Brigands to clamber inside.

While the overalled worker sprinted to a little wooden hut and barricaded himself in, the driver of the parked tanker started his engine. Outside, Darrell Snubs arrived in a four-wheel drive piloted by Oluchi. He hopped out as a pair of camera operators recorded his every move.

'This is sensational! Sensational! We are filming live!' Snubs blurted to the camera. He had crazy eyes and looked like he'd been in a war, with blood from his injured neck streaked down his tattooed chest.

While the Brigands headed for the tanker, desperate to yank the driver from his cab before he could get it moving, Robin opened the driver's door of the Ranger truck. He coughed violently as he breathed the powdery residue from the airbag explosions. Mr Khan had his eyes open, but seemed dazed. Robin used his pocket knife to burst a partly inflated airbag, then leaned across to undo Khan's seatbelt.

'You OK, sir?' Robin asked.

'Bashed knee and ripped trousers,' Khan said as Robin helped him climb out.

Robin couldn't help smiling. 'You're a thousand times cooler than I thought you were, sir,' he admitted.

Khan gave Robin one of his stiff looks, but before he could issue any words of wisdom, a massive Rottweiler guard dog pounced on Khan's back and knocked him to the ground.

'Where did that come from?' Robin gasped, shooting frightened glances in all directions as he heard barking and realised that someone inside had unleashed a pack of guard dogs.

Luke was the fastest of the four Brigands. He escaped the dogs, threw the driver out of the parked tanker and climbed into the cab. Ratbreath wasn't so lucky. He curled up in the dirt as a jet-black Doberman buried its teeth in the arm of his leather jacket.

As Luke made a quick study of the tanker's controls, Robin saw that it wouldn't have room to get through without smashing the crippled Forest Ranger truck wedged between them. Then he glanced back towards the main road and saw that Mr Khan had fought off the dog, only for it to keep going and attack Darrell Snubs.

Snubs squealed at his camera operator as the huge salivating beast tried to bite his bare chest. 'Don't film it, you idiot. Pull this damned dog off me!'

But neither Oluchi nor the camera operator had any desire to tangle with the powerful dog.

'I'll be scarred for life!' Snubs wailed. 'Get this monster off me!'

Robin knew it wasn't the dog's fault that humans had trained it to bite people. He pulled an arrow from his backpack, but snapped off the sharp metal tip before aiming at the dog's rear end. He wasn't sure if the arrow would make the huge dog run off or just make it even angrier, but he had to try.

Luckily for Snubs, the dog yelped and shot off down the road. Luke blasted the giant air horn inside the tanker, giving Robin a fright.

'Coming through,' Luke shouted out of the driver's window as he lined the truck up.

'That beast bit my nipple off!' Snubs sobbed, as Oluchi and a couple of TV people helped him back to his feet and into the four-wheel drive.

Robin realised that his dirt bike would get flattened when the Ranger truck got knocked sideways.

He was wary of getting closer to the gate because there were at least two more guard dogs on the prowl, but he gave Luke a *wait up* hand signal and quickly straddled his bike.

Mr Khan had limped into the back of the four-wheel drive with Snubs and Oluchi, but as Robin prepared to drive off, he saw the fearless camera operator Daisy scramble through the twisted gate in front of the tanker.

'You went inside,' Robin gasped. 'With those dogs!'

He was a thrill-seeker, but that seemed too much even for him.

'It was worth it for the footage I got,' Daisy yelled exuberantly as Oluchi pulled away in the truck, tailed by a couple of TV vans that had just arrived. 'I could win an award! This is the greatest day of my life.'

'Just get on the back,' Robin urged.

Daisy was breathing heavily, sweat dripping off her brow onto the back of Robin's neck, as she straddled the bike and locked one arm around his waist.

'Wait for the truck to move, then drive off slowly,' she told Robin, as a Brigand shot past on his Harley and Luke gave another impatient blast of the tanker's horn. 'I have to film that tanker smashing up the Ranger truck and bursting onto the road.'

Robin was sick of pandering to TV cameras, but Daisy's reckless enthusiasm was infectious, and the more spectacular the TV footage looked, the more people would see that Guy Gisborne wasn't someone they wanted as their new sheriff.

Luke groaned and honked again when Daisy swung the camera to point back at his truck. Robin did what Daisy asked, gently twisting the accelerator when Luke floored the gas pedal. This kept Robin close enough for Daisy to record the sparks and grinding metal as the remains of the gates tore away and the two-tonne Ranger truck got obliterated by fifty tons of tanker.

As Robin sped up and turned onto the road, Daisy slowly swung the camera around to film the bike's handlebars and the back of Robin's head. His messy hair flapped wildly as the dirt bike sped towards the setting sun.

38. CHOCOLATE DIGESTIVE KIND OF GUY

While Robin did his best not to get shot, kidnapped or crushed by a tanker, Alan and Josie had spent a more sedate afternoon inside the Nest. Their job was to manage a team keeping close tabs on Guy Gisborne.

This involved tracking devices fitted to three of Gisborne's cars, plus messages and appointment data from Gisborne Waste Management's hacked email system. On the streets of Locksley, a dozen rebels and staff from Darrell Snubs' production company kept eyes on Gisborne's home, office and some other places where he regularly hung out.

Three hours after Luke stole the tanker filled with surplus paint, Rebel security officer Ísbjörg and her boyfriend were tucking into vegan burgers as Guy Gisborne exited the private upstairs lounge of Wally's Steakhouse. He looked tired and a little wobbly from three rum and Cokes.

Ísbjörg tapped out a message to the Nest:

```
GISBORNE LEAVING
LOOKS DRUNK
NO BODYGUARD
```

A golf-ball-sized camera attached to the windscreen of a parked car filmed Gisborne dropping his keys as he stumbled across the puddled parking lot to his pimped-out Mercedes G-Wagon.

Back at the Nest, Josie read Ísbjörg's message. She waited for the tracking device to show her which way Gisborne was driving, then called Oluchi.

'Gisborne's leaving Wally's,' Josie told her. 'I'm sure he's heading home, but I'll confirm when he pulls onto the North Cross Route.'

Oluchi, Robin and the TV crew had spent the past three hours in a brightly lit warehouse. It had originally been home to a production line for a frozen pizza company, but it now housed Darrell Snubs' giant silver motorhome, a dozen vehicles rented by his production company and, most importantly, the stolen tanker.

Brigands had given the tanker some minor repairs after its dramatic exit from the landfill site, while rebels had attached banners down each side.

One banner had a giant picture of Heirani Amo with her brother Max and the words *KILLED BY GUY*

GISBORNE. The other side of the tanker had the words *INVESTIGATE NOW* and a link to an online video, with footage of the damaged metal cabin where the explosion took place and an interview where Jeanne the engineer talked about how Mile End Landfill was leaking methane gas and could possibly explode.

Muddy, tired-looking camera operators, technicians and runners looked up from their phones as Robin announced the latest news.

'Looks like Gisborne's driving himself home,' Robin shouted, as he glanced about looking for Snubs. 'Where's Darrell at?'

A set with cameras, lights and the stolen tanker in the background had been set up to film what happened next. Snubs could have used the three-hour wait to shower and change into one of the many outfits in his trailer, but he'd decided that his show would look more exciting if he stayed in his muddy clothes.

After receiving first-aid treatment for a couple of small, but nasty, dog bites, Snubs had asked Larry the make-up guy to dress the wounds in huge white bandages and told him to leave the crusted blood around his neck.

'Showtime!' Snubs told his crew excitedly. 'Let's nail this dirtbag.'

As Snubs settled on a bar stool in front of three video lights, Larry touched up the comedian's make-up, while a runner handed him an old-fashioned flip phone and explained that he had to press and hold zero on the keypad to dial the number.

'Quiet, everyone, phones to silent! Go lights, go cameras one and four,' Paul the director ordered. 'We only get one shot at this.'

Everyone in the warehouse watched tensely as Darrell put the phone on speaker and dialled.

'Who is this?' Guy Gisborne snapped.

Snubs spoke with a cheesy fake charm. 'My name is Darrell Snubs. Am I speaking with Guy Gisborne?'

'Snubs?' Gisborne said, confused. 'Who are you? This is my private line. How did you get this number?'

'I have my ways,' Snubs oozed, as he showed his perfect teeth to the camera.

'You're that comedian who wears the stupid waistcoats.'

Snubs laughed. 'That's me, Mr Gisborne. I've heard you're running for sheriff and I just wanted to ask a few questions.'

Gisborne grunted irritably, but he was desperate to win his sheriff's election campaign so his tone changed to calm and professional. 'OK, Mr Snubs, how can I help you—'

'Do call me Darrell,' Snubs interrupted, giving the camera a cheeky glance.

'Darrell,' Gisborne said. 'I have a full schedule. Can I suggest that you set up an interview? You'll need to speak with my press officer Caroline in the morning.'

'This is a rather pressing matter,' Snubs said. 'I've received information that paint and other chemical substances are being illegally dumped at your South Range landfill site. My researchers have emails that you sent about the matter, and a recording of three phone calls you made to Katerina at your waste management—'

Gisborne's anger simmered beneath his attempt to sound like a politician. 'My waste management companies meet the highest international standards for recycling and environmental protection. Now, I don't know how you got hold of my private number, but if you wish to discuss this matter further you need to call my press officer Caroline at the Locksley campaign office.'

Gisborne sounded like he was about to end the call, so Snubs spoke super fast. 'But PLEASE! Mr Gisborne, I happen to be in your neighbourhood this evening. I'm a few minutes from your house and I've been told you're driving home. Could I just drop by and straighten this whole thing out?'

'How do you know where I am?' Gisborne snapped.

'I'm happy to bring biscuits,' Snubs joked. 'Are you a fruit shortcake or a chocolate digestive kind of guy?'

'You're having me followed?'

'I am a guy who knows a lot of things about you,' Snubs said cockily.

'You want to be careful about any allegations you make,' Gisborne growled. 'I have a lot of friends in this town.'

Snubs laughed. 'Was that a threat, Mr Gisborne? You really don't want me to drop by your house with a packet of delicious biscuits?'

Gisborne grunted and hung up his phone. Snubs snapped the flip phone shut and looked directly into the camera.

'Well, viewers, it seems that Mr Gisborne didn't want me to visit his house, but do you know what? I think we're going to do that anyway.'

39. BLACK BESS II

Gisborne looked spooked as he sat behind the wheel of the deafening 800-horsepower customised Mercedes G-Wagon that he'd named Black Bess II. He considered abandoning his drive home and going back to Wally's or his office in town. But he was worried about his wife.

'Dawn,' Gisborne said sharply when she answered the phone. 'That dumbass comedian Darrell Snubs is on my back. If anyone comes near the house before I get home, *don't* open the gate, *don't* answer the door. Better still, turn out the lights so it looks like nobody's home.'

The road was dark as Gisborne took a long look in his rear-view mirror to see if he was being tailed. Then he called his political campaign manager to see if she had any idea why a stand-up comedian was interested in his waste management company. But it was late and the call went to voicemail.

'When you get this message, call me right back!' Gisborne shouted.

He called Locksley's Chief of Police next, telling her to gather up every spare officer and send them to his house as soon as possible. Then he called up one of his nastiest thugs and made the same request.

'Remember I'm running for sheriff. Make sure you smash *all* their cameras before teaching them a lesson.'

Gisborne glanced warily in all directions as Black Bess II pulled up at the heavy front gate of his North Locksley home. The large, modern house stood behind high walls on a three-acre plot. There was an elaborate marble fountain on the driveway and a line of five luxury cars at the grand front entrance.

Everything felt normal as Gisborne waited for the electronic gate to open. As he rolled up the short gravel driveway, he saw his wife, Dawn, peeking out of an upstairs window dressed in her yoga gear.

Gisborne opened his side window to give her a reassuring wave, then pushed the button on the little box clipped to his sun visor to close the gate. But instead of closing, the gate jerked and clanked.

Gisborne began to suspect that something was about to go down. He gave the button another push, but got the same useless clank.

A few hours earlier Katerina Kendall had called him to talk about a bizarre call she'd taken from a confused and babbling landfill site worker, who said that he'd been forced to barricade himself in his hut while a gang of

Brigands hijacked a tanker truck waiting to dump its load at South Range landfill site.

They'd both brushed off the theft, because although smashing through a gate and stealing a tanker truck in broad daylight was odd, the Brigands were notoriously erratic and one of their main sources of income was stealing vehicles, stripping them down and selling the spare parts.

But now Darrell Snubs knew about the paint in the stolen truck. The comedian also mentioned that he'd read emails, listened to private phone conversations, and even knew that Gisborne was on his way home.

As these facts came together in Gisborne's head, he saw signs of a complex plan. Though he had many enemies, the rebels at Sherwood Castle were the only ones capable of putting together something this sophisticated. While the hacking stuff meant that the person he hated most in the whole world was involved . . .

'Robin Hood, that little turd!' Guy Gisborne thundered to himself as he jumped out of Black Bess II and smashed the door shut.

Gisborne considered walking down the drive to close the sabotaged gate manually. But was that exactly what the rebels hoped he'd do?

Instead, he ran the other way to his front door, shuddering with fear as he imagined Robin Hood sitting in a nearby tree, an arrow aimed at his back.

Anxiety had mostly sobered Gisborne up, but he still fumbled and dropped his keys again as he tugged them out of his cluttered jacket pocket. As he bent down to pick them up, he sensed the headlight beams and clattering diesel engine of a tanker truck that had just turned into his street.

Before the key was in Gisborne's front door, the growling tanker had swerved through the open gate onto his front drive. Luke judged the corner badly and knocked bricks out of Gisborne's front wall. Then he swerved around the fountain and came to a gravel-spitting halt with the hiss of hydraulic brakes, the truck's big front grille less than thirty centimetres from Gisborne's matt-black Ferrari.

The rebels' next move had been carefully choreographed and practised several times while the stolen tanker waited in the warehouse. Video lights strapped along both sides of the tanker were switched on by remote control. Camera and sound operators jumped out of a production van that had arrived behind the tanker, and an aerial photography team hiding in the neighbour's garden launched a pair of camera drones to get overhead shots.

'I've called the cops!' Gisborne shouted towards the tanker as he tried opening his front door, only to find that whoever sabotaged his front gate had also filled his front door lock with fast-setting glue. 'Wait and see what happens when you're locked in a police cell!'

Robin Hood and Darrell Snubs arrived next, in a people carrier driven by Oluchi. As three camera operators and two drones filmed, the pair ran to the rear of the tanker, clambered up the narrow access ladder leading to the roof, then jogged along the top until they reached the cab.

Snubs had stuck with his bloodied action hero look, but Robin had chosen to play it safe and wore a combat helmet and a ballistic vest.

'You won't get away with this,' Gisborne shouted as he squirmed in his front doorway, shielding his eyes from the blazing video lights.

'How's your balls, Gisborne?' Robin asked cheerfully. 'The one I didn't shoot off the last time we met.'

'How's your daddy doing in jail?' Gisborne taunted back. 'Are you gonna kill me? You still haven't got the guts.'

'It wouldn't be hard from this distance.' Robin snorted and looked over his shoulder at his bow. 'But unlike some people I could name, I'm not a cold-blooded murderer.'

'And not in front of the cameras,' Darrell Snubs added, desperate not to let Robin upstage him. 'I already explained on the phone, Mr G. I just want a chat.'

'Whatever,' Gisborne spat.

'I wanted to ask you about this tanker I'm standing on. The fifty thousand litres of toxic paint that's inside it, and the phone calls I've heard, where you talk to Katerina Kendall about illegally disposing of two tankers of surplus paint as a favour to Sir Stanley Launcelot.'

Gisborne squirmed in the dazzling lights, but all he could think to say was a pathetic, 'You are on private property.'

'As a well-known comedian, activist and national treasure, I can't be involved in any criminal activity,' Darrell Snubs announced rather formally to the cameras, as he held his hands in the air. 'I am documenting this situation and neither myself nor my production company are in any way responsible for what is about to happen. Though I do reserve the right to laugh my ass off.'

As Snubs spoke these words, which his lawyers hoped would keep him and his production company from getting sued for damages, Robin lay down on the tanker roof, reached into the gap between the tanker and its articulated truck, then twisted a release valve and pulled a big orange lever.

40. DARRELL THE MAGNIFICENT

The lever Robin pulled opened up two large circular ports, one on each side of the tanker. To maximise damage, the rebels had connected these to manure-spreading attachments, donated by a local farmer who Gisborne was trying to kick off his land to create another trash dump. These enabled paint to shoot twenty metres in a wide, spinning arc.

The jets of magnolia paint caught the bright video lights, creating a dazzling toxic fountain on either side of the tanker. Robin only got spattered by fine particles of paint as he stood up and sprinted along the top of the tanker to the ladder at the back, but Gisborne took a blasting and was blind and furious as he pulled his coat up over his head and stumbled frantically away.

Black Bess II and the other five luxury cars on Gisborne's driveway were saturated in seconds, while the entire front of his house soon wore enough paint sludge to look like a modern art masterpiece.

Unknown to the rebels, the paint had spent years in metal cans, and this deterioration had resulted in lumps of rust big enough to crack garden planters, break windows and trash a conservatory.

'That paint stinks,' Robin complained as he slid down the ladder on the back of the tanker.

He laughed triumphantly as he stumbled into Oluchi, giving her a celebratory hug while one of the camera operators filmed.

'Shame we only got one tanker,' Robin told her. 'But I think we've made our point.'

'We need to clear out before the cops arrive,' Oluchi told Robin. 'Especially you.'

'Your plan rocked!' Luke told Oluchi, as he joined Robin behind the tanker.

'Looks like you caught some,' Robin told Luke, as he noticed paint spatters over the young Brigand's back.

'I jumped out of the cab and thought I'd run clear, but that paint was mental,' Luke explained exuberantly. 'Some of that gunk is catching the wind, going clear over the house and landing in the swimming pool out back.'

'House is wrecked, cars are wrecked,' Robin shouted cheerfully. 'But where's Darrell? I thought he was behind me.'

Robin spun back towards the tanker, fearing that Darrell had slipped off the tanker's roof and fallen into the blasting paint. But as he backed down Gisborne's driveway towards the road, Robin saw Darrell atop the tanker. One of the drones hovered over the comedian's head and he mugged off for the camera, thumping his bloody chest, punching the air and shouting the name of his new show.

'*Truth to Power! Truth to Pow-ahhhhhh!*'

'Snubs is a knob,' Luke noted, then yanked Robin by the side of his flak jacket. 'Time to leave. You're riding with me, and Cut-Throat said he'd chop my thumbs off if I let you get busted.'

Robin had wanted to keep riding his own bike, but it was fully dark now and after seeing his unimpressive riding skills earlier in the day, Ratbreath and another Brigand who was better not argued with decided that Robin should escape as the passenger of a more experienced rider.

'See you back at the castle,' Robin told Oluchi, rubbing his stinging eye.

TV folks had unloaded Robin's getaway bike, but before he could put on his helmet, he got distracted by a sudden drop in noise levels.

Fifty thousand litres of paint had run through the muck-spreading gear, leaving just occasional burbles from the sprayer nozzles. Darrell Snubs finally strode to the rear of the tanker, holding his arms aloft and bowing to the cameras as if he'd done it all by himself.

'Darrell, stop showing off,' Paul the director shouted angrily. 'Gisborne owns Locksley PD. They may not be able to charge us with any crime, but they'll kick the snot out of us.'

'I can take anything!' Snubs boasted as he reached the metal ladder. 'I survived bandits and dog bites. I am Darrell Snubs. I am the magnificent one!'

Luke started the bike as Robin finally pulled on his helmet. There was a bang. Robin thought the bike had misfired, but all the TV folks started screaming and taking cover.

'Snubs is shot! Snubs is shot!' someone screamed.

As Robin looked up Gisborne's driveway, he saw paint trails running everywhere while TV people rushed towards Snubs, who'd fallen off the back of the empty tanker.

'He's shot!' Paul the director shouted as he dived to the ground in front of Snubs. 'Someone call an ambulance.'

Robin glanced up at the house, where Dawn Gisborne stood on her paint-spattered bedroom balcony. She had the same angry expression as her daughter Clare, and she held a sniper rifle with a sophisticated laser scope.

'You ruined my house, Snubs,' Dawn shouted. 'Now I've ruined you.'

A little camera drone whizzed down and hovered in front of Dawn Gisborne. She aimed the green dot of her laser scope and blasted it out of the sky. Robin was instinctively drawn towards the action, and reached behind for an arrow. But when he tried stepping off the bike, Luke grabbed his backpack.

'She'll shoot you next,' Luke warned Robin, as the first police sirens sounded in the distance. 'Now get on the damned bike.'

There was nothing Robin could do to help Snubs. Since Luke was four times his size, he did what he was told, settling back on the saddle, gripping the young Brigand around the waist, and letting him open the throttle and blaze out of Dodge before the cops showed up.

41. THE NEW PRESENTER

'Why is my living room full of kids?' Karma yelled, as she stepped into the penthouse lounge at five to nine the following morning. 'You lot will miss the start of school!'

Besides Karma and Indio's own kids, the giant projector screen in the penthouse lounge had drawn a crowd that included most of Matt and Finn's mates, along with Alan, Josie and three of her friends.

Normally it took a birthday party or a new superhero movie to get this many Sherwood Castle kids in one place, but now they were glued to the morning news. As presenter Lynn Hoapili spoke, the scrolling ticker along the bottom of the screen highlighted the latest developments:

- DOCTORS SAY DARRELL SNUBS' CONDITION IS SERIOUS BUT STABLE
- LOCKSLEY POLICE RELEASE DAWN GISBORNE WITHOUT CHARGE, SAY SHE WAS ACTING IN SELF DEFENCE

- DAMAGE TO GUY GISBORNE'S CARS AND HOME
  ESTIMATED TO BE IN EXCESS OF £3 MILLION
- VIDEO OF HOOD/SNUBS PAINT ATTACK RECEIVES
  FIFTY MILLION VIEWS IN TWELVE HOURS
- ENVIRONMENTAL GROUPS AND CAPITAL
  CITY MAYOR DEMAND A FULL GOVERNMENT
  INVESTIGATION INTO GISBORNE WASTE
  MANAGEMENT

A cheer rippled across the penthouse lounge when the big screen cut to a shot of Oluchi. She stood outside Locksley General hospital holding a microphone.

'That lady was in the Nest with Robin all last week,' one little lad blurted, only to get a contemptuous shove from his big sister.

'Everyone knows, Kevin. Shut your gob!'

Up on the big screen, presenter Lynn Hoapili explained what was going on. 'I am now live with Oluchi Thomas. She spent yesterday with Darrell Snubs' team, documenting the Sherwood Forest rebels' spectacular assault on Guy Gisborne's home, and she personally witnessed the shooting incident. Oluchi, what's the latest from Locksley General?'

Oluchi answered in her most professional TV presenter voice. 'Less than ten minutes ago, we saw a medical helicopter lift off from the hospital rooftop. We understand that Darrell Snubs and two critical care nurses were on board.'

'Has there been an update on Snubs' condition?' Lynn asked.

'Darrell Snubs' spokesperson released a statement, saying that he is on his way to a hospital in Liverpool. As soon as the chopper lands, a team of specialist trauma surgeons will operate to remove a bullet fragment lodged dangerously close to his spine,' Oluchi explained. 'The spokesperson did not take questions and gave little information about Snubs' current state. We don't know if he is conscious, but we believe he would not have been allowed to leave in a helicopter if his condition was life-threatening.'

'And with Darrell Snubs out of action, I understand that you have taken on the task of presenting this week's episode of *Truth to Power*,' Lynn said.

Oluchi tried hard not to smile about her rapid promotion, from wannabe journalist to lead presenter on a prime-time show that would draw a record-breaking audience.

'I'm honoured to have been given the opportunity to infiltrate the Sherwood Forest rebels and tell this story,' Oluchi told her former boss. 'I spoke with *Truth to Power*'s producers late last night. They considered postponing this week's episode until Darrell was well enough to present the show himself, but with so much media interest after the shooting, we decided it was more important to let viewers see the episode now.'

The news channel cut away from Oluchi to Lynn in the studio. 'And you'll be able to watch this sensational breaking story, featuring Robin Hood, Darrell Snubs and incredible unreleased footage of last night's shooting, right here on Channel Fourteen this coming Saturday.

'In the next half hour, we'll have live footage as Darrell Snubs' helicopter lands at the Liverpool University Hospital, but first here's Dok-Mai with a weather update.'

The screen in the penthouse lounge went blank and twenty kids groaned as they looked around and saw Karma holding the remote.

'Get downstairs to school!' she ordered. 'The lot of you.'

Matt looked furious. 'Mum, you're so uncool,' he moaned. 'The guys are waiting to see the clip where Mr Khan smashes through the gate.'

'You've seen it six times already,' Karma said, as she rolled up a puzzle magazine and used it to gently swat some little kids sitting cross-legged on the floor. 'You've been watching that channel since you got up two hours ago. And don't come whingeing to me if you all get detention from Mr Khan for being late.'

'I bet Khan won't be at school today.' Matt snorted.

Josie nodded and laughed as she got off the carpet. 'Robin says Mr Khan borrowed three trucks from his pals in the Forest Rangers. Now he's got to explain why two have bullet holes and the third is a mangled wreck.'

'That's worse than the time Robin accidentally shot the door mirror off my mum's BMW,' Alan said, glancing around like something was missing. 'Speaking of golden boy, did Robin sneak down to school without us?'

'Robin went to the toilet,' Josie said, as she pointed out Robin's school backpack on one of the sofas.

'But that was yonks ago,' Alan noted, while Karma stewarded more sluggish kids out of her lounge. 'He must be doing an absolutely epic dump.'

'There's a mental image I can live without!' Josie said, grimacing.

Matt was the last of the younger kids to pick up his school stuff and head down to school. Karma sighed as she surveyed the carpet, which was overrun with cushions, cups, sweet wrappers and cereal bowls. Then she looked at Josie and Alan.

'Why are you two still lurking?' she asked, as she tapped an imaginary watch on her wrist.

Josie took Robin's school pack then marched to his bedroom with Alan and Karma in tow. The bathroom door was locked, so she thumped on it.

'Robin, are you OK in there?' she yelled.

Alan grinned. 'Have you got violent explosive diarrhoea again?'

'Or did your ego get so swollen that you can't get your massive head through the door?' Josie added, joining Alan's laughter.

'Quiet, you idiots, I'm on the phone,' Robin yelled back.

A minute later Robin twisted the bolt and stepped out, flicking water off his wet hands and smiling.

'My dad's lawyer, Tybalt, called,' Robin explained excitedly. 'The judge has scheduled the appeal hearing for eleven o'clock. If they win, my dad could get out of prison *today*!'

'Nice one,' Alan said, as Josie smiled and held up two sets of crossed fingers.

But Karma worried that Robin would be upset if things went badly. 'That's great news, but let's see what happens, eh? Don't set your hopes too high.'

'I know,' Robin agreed. 'If Dad's not released, Tybalt says he'll sneak me into the courthouse to see him before he's sent back to Pelican Island. Either way, I'll have to miss school if I'm going into town.'

'What!' Alan complained. 'Again?'

'Mr Khan won't like that,' Josie added.

Karma glared at the pair of them. 'Why are you two still here? Grab your school stuff and scram!'

Robin couldn't resist childishly poking his tongue out at his friend and girlfriend as they left his room.

'Enjoy School Zone,' he teased. 'It's sure to be super fun.'

Karma turned her glare on Robin.

'Nobody will stop you going into Locksley to see what happens with your dad,' she said, as she wagged a stern finger. 'But don't get cocky, because I'll make sure you catch up on all your schoolwork this weekend.'

42. BACK IN FASHION

It took an hour to get Robin and two bodyguards from Sherwood Castle to the parking lot behind a shuttered frozen yoghurt store at the edge of the forest. He was picked up by an elegantly dressed, well-spoken young woman named Zoe.

She was one of many brilliant, principled law graduates who wanted to boost their careers by working as unpaid interns for the crusading lawyer Tybalt Bull. Though her giant red Porsche coupé and designer heels suggested that her quest for social justice had the backing of some seriously rich parents.

'Tybalt sent me, since I'm the last person anyone would expect to have Robin Hood hiding in her car,' Zoe explained.

As Robin threw his bow and backpack on the rear seat and slid onto the quilted white leather, he noticed a pen and two blank birthday cards on the armrest.

'I hope you don't mind me asking,' Zoe said as she buckled her seatbelt. 'My twin sisters are your biggest fans. They have nothing in common, apart from their unicorn hoodies and Robin Hood posters on their bedroom walls. They turn twelve next week, and if you could write them birthday cards they will literally explode!'

'No worries,' Robin said, feeling a little embarrassed and wondering what messages to write, while Zoe gave his two bodyguards a wave and pulled out onto a busy road. 'My handwriting is messy, I'm afraid.'

'It's not just my sisters who think you're cool,' Zoe continued. 'The world is full of people who complain. But how many stand up and do something, like you? One in a thousand? One in a million?'

Zoe was a chatterbox, and kept going for the entire twenty-minute drive to Locksley. She told Robin how everyone had been talking about him in the seafood restaurant she'd dined at the night before.

'People kept saying Robin Hood was last summer's fad,' Zoe gushed. 'But after yesterday, you're trending everywhere. I was supposed to be meeting five friends on Saturday night, but two have already dropped out because they want to stay home and watch *Truth to Power*.'

As her electric Porsche sped towards central Locksley, Zoe told Robin that she wasn't interested in money, that she'd rather die than end up working in a dull corporate law office like her mother, and how she really wanted to get a poodle but couldn't look after it properly because Tybalt kept her working twelve to fifteen hours a day.

Robin slid down low in his seat when they hit traffic and unusually crowded pavements near the town centre. The coupé's rear windows were heavily tinted, so he felt safe peeking out when they stopped to let a noisy crowd of university students cross in front of them.

Many covered their faces with bandanas, fearing that Locksley cops might hunt them down later. Two wore *Robin Hood Lives* hoodies and several held up placards with slogans like *Free Ardagh*, *End Police Corruption NOW* and *Don't Vote For Gangsters*.

Robin's favourite was a group of goth students, who'd dressed a shop dummy as Guy Gisborne and dragged it by a noose around its neck.

'Quite a turnout,' Robin said.

Zoe nodded as the traffic cleared ahead. 'Locksley Uni students have really got into the campaign to free your dad. They're utterly sick of getting shaken down by cops who want bribes, or putting up with Gisborne's thuggish club doormen and drug dealers when they go out on the town.'

Robin risked another peek out of the window as they reached the edge of Civic Square, home to the town's Central Court, town hall, and a crumbling museum and art gallery.

He was impressed to see hundreds of his dad's supporters gathered along metal police barriers lined up in front of Locksley Central Court. A looser group mingled around the statue of Sir Edward Locksley in the square's centre, including teens in purple Locksley High polo shirts and old folks with a big banner that claimed Gisborne had ripped off their pensions.

Zoe steered her bulky Porsche through the tight entrance of a multi-storey parking lot. Robin realised that he should have climbed over the back seat and hidden in the trunk when a court security officer tapped on the driver's-side window. Luckily, Zoe's upmarket car and posh accent meant the officer barely glanced at her Central Court ID badge before waving her through.

'Be careful if you go out on the street, pet,' the officer warned. 'There's student scumbags everywhere.'

'I'll bear that in mind, officer,' Zoe said, annoyed but careful to hide it.

After driving up a dozen tight ramps, the Porsche broke into winter sunshine on the roof of the parking lot. As Zoe pulled into a charging bay, Robin saw that the only other car on this level was covered in bird crap and had no wheels.

'It never gets busy up here,' Zoe explained, as she skimmed through some messages she'd missed while driving. 'But it's still safest if you stay out of sight in the trunk. I've put pillows and a torch back there and I'll leave it open a crack so you get fresh air.'

Robin smiled as he folded the opposite half of the rear seat and peered into a cosy little den lined with a picnic blanket.

'That's five-star luxury,' he told Zoe. 'I usually have to hide in trunks full of rusty tools and smelly boots.'

'I'm glad you approve,' Zoe said as she glanced at her watch. 'The last message I got said that the judge was on schedule and your dad's hearing was about to start. So, keep your fingers crossed and with any luck you won't be hiding back there for long.'

43. VILE LITTLE HOOLIGAN

After twenty minutes in the trunk of Zoe's Porsche, Robin started hearing more noise from the protests down at street level. There were chants, jeers, police sirens and regular PA announcements ordering the crowd to move back from the barriers in front of the courthouse.

Robin tried to watch the TV news on his phone, but his signal was weak and the picture kept breaking up. He had better luck streaming a local news radio station. They interviewed a spokesperson from Locksley police who wanted everyone to stay away from Civic Square, then a bunch of people demonstrating inside the square called the radio station, urging everyone to come into town and join the protests.

Robin laughed as he listened to an elderly caller ranting about how young people needed more discipline. Then the caller read out a list of crimes Robin had committed and told listeners that he was a vile little hooligan who deserved to be thrown in jail until his hair turned grey.

Less amusing was a woman caller who said she'd be voting for Guy Gisborne in the upcoming sheriff elections because he was a local man who was tough and knew how to get things done, even if that meant bending a few rules.

As the radio cut to an advert for Mindy Burger's new range of frosted mini-donuts, Robin was jolted by two bangs loud enough to make the Porsche's dashboard rattle. These were followed by screaming.

Desperate to know what had happened, Robin peeked out through the crack in the car's trunk to make sure the coast was clear. Then he rolled out, crept around the side of the car and squatted, looking between the bars of the metal railing that edged the parking lot.

Central Court and a couple of other buildings partially blocked his view of Civic Square, but he still saw groups of people scattering as clouds of light grey tear gas wafted towards them.

But while some protestors tried to back out of the square, coughing, their eyes burning, the side streets were busy with protestors trying to get in. In some spots they were held back by police barriers, but in others there was nothing to stop them.

'This is an unlicensed gathering!' the square's PA system screeched. 'Leave the Civic Square in an orderly fashion, or you will be arrested.'

Robin felt queasy as Locksley police released more grenades filled with stinging tear gas. The tangle of people fleeing while others tried to enter the square had caused several falls and tramplings. Nobody was seriously hurt, but that was surely only a matter of time.

'Civic Square is now closed!' the PA screeched, while a line of masked student protestors lobbed water bottles, eggs and anything else that came to hand towards lines of cops in riot gear. 'Anyone remaining in the square will receive a heavy fine and a criminal record.'

Robin got another jolt as someone directly behind him yelled, 'Hey!'

He spun with his bow, but it was Zoe, looking annoyed.

'You were supposed to stay in the car,' she said irritably as she unplugged her car from the charging terminal. 'Lucky it was me who snuck up on you.'

'I could have shot them,' Robin said defensively.

Zoe was too busy to argue. 'The main court entrance on Civic Square is completely blocked off. Tybalt wants me to drive around to the entrance at the side and be ready for a possible pick-up. The appeal judge has retired to her chambers. She could come out and deliver her verdict at any minute.'

'What about me?' Robin asked.

Zoe pointed to the trunk. 'Unless you plan to walk home.'

'Right,' Robin said. 'Did you get any vibes? Does Tybalt think Dad's appeal is gonna go our way?'

Zoe shrugged as she shut Robin back in the trunk, then opened the driver's door. 'Interns like me drive people around and make photocopies. Tybalt doesn't confide in me. Either your dad—'

Zoe stopped speaking because there were three sharp bangs as Locksley police unleashed more tear gas canisters.

'Someone's gonna get killed down there,' Zoe yelled furiously as she buckled her seatbelt. 'There's no need for the cops to gas a peaceful crowd.'

'I hate Locksley police,' Robin shouted from the trunk as Zoe began reversing out of the parking bay. 'What did you start saying about my dad?'

'It's fifty metres between the court your dad's in and the side entrance,' Zoe explained. 'If Tybalt steps outside on his own, we lost the appeal. If your dad's with him, we can start smiling.'

44. THE CANDIDATE

It was a two-hundred-metre drive from the exit of the multi-storey car park to the side entrance of Locksley Central Courthouse. But the journey was a crawl through streets packed with people.

Gassed protestors squatted at the roadside with garish red eyes and snot streaming from their noses. Even shielded in the trunk of the car, Robin caught a peppery tang in his throat and a slight sting in his eyes.

None of the protestors knew who Zoe was, or that Robin was hiding in her trunk. They just saw the type of fancy car that would be driven by a rich businessperson or a dodgy lawyer, and expressed their contempt by thumping on the hood and aiming half-drunk lattes at the windscreen.

The tension ratcheted further as Zoe stopped in front of a line of cops. She flashed her court access pass and tried to explain that she had to get to the side of the court to pick up a defendant.

'Posh bird like you, working for Tybalt Bull,' one cop sneered from behind his riot helmet. 'Are you having a laugh?'

Zoe looked stressed as she got out of her car and unsuccessfully tried to catch the attention of a senior officer behind the line of riot cops. Then she got back behind the wheel, sent a message to Tybalt and kept sounding her horn until a senior court official finally came over and ordered the cops to let her through.

The road at the side of Central Court had police barricades at both ends, while most protestors who'd braved the barrages of tear gas remained at the court's front entrance. But Tybalt had tipped off the media about his plan to exit via the side, and a gaggle of photographers and TV crews waited patiently as Zoe's red Porsche rolled up behind them.

As minutes passed, the sun hitting the outside of the trunk made Robin's back sweat while the lingering tear gas made his eyes itch.

Outside the car, protestors who'd spotted the media pack began to realise what was happening and moved their focus from the front of the courthouse to the blockades at each end of the side street. And while the cops had plenty of tear gas left, they were wary of gassing photographers and TV crews and creating a storm of bad publicity.

'Finally,' Zoe told Robin, as the court door opened. 'It's happening.'

'My dad there?' Robin blurted, desperate to crawl out and see for himself, but knowing it was too risky with cops nearby.

'Ardagh!' Zoe said, her voice rising to a squeal and cracking a huge smile. 'We bloody did it!'

Robin felt his eyes flood with tears. 'Heck, yes!' he said, then kicked the back of the seat out of sheer excitement. 'Is Dad coming towards us?'

'Tybalt has stopped at the top of the steps by the exit,' Zoe explained. 'Your dad and Little John are there too. About fifty people are taking photos, and the protestors at the end of the street are rocking the metal barriers.'

Robin heard the crowd roar as they spotted Ardagh Hood on the court steps.

'What's Tybalt saying?' Robin asked.

'Can't hear,' Zoe said, then Robin remembered the local radio stream on his phone.

He turned up the volume and was pleased that they were running a live feed of Tybalt speaking on the steps less than twenty metres away.

'. . . appeal judge has accepted Ardagh Hood's petition for acquittal on the grounds that police did not follow proper procedures after his arrest,' Tybalt said dryly. 'My client pleaded guilty to theft charges, which cannot be appealed, but the judge has agreed that Ardagh Hood's sentence will be reduced to time served. Therefore, my client has been released from the remainder of his prison sentence, subject to a good behaviour bond.'

Outside the car, Robin heard metal barriers clatter as protestors broke through, chanting Ardagh's name.

'Mr Hood, how does it feel to be a free man?' one of the journalists shouted, as another tripped on the steps and dropped his microphone.

'These first six minutes have been good!' Ardagh shouted back, getting a few laughs.

Tybalt spoke more formally. 'My client, Ardagh Hood, now has a brief announcement to make.'

'First of all, I would like to thank Tybalt Bull and his team, who have worked incredibly hard to secure my release from prison,' Ardagh began, as the crowd of cheering protestors reached the bottom of the steps and began jostling the camera crews and journalists.

'I went to prison because I stood up to a nasty, criminal bully named Guy Gisborne. My time in prison has only increased my determination to keep up this fight. Since Gisborne is now running for election as Sheriff of Nottingham, I have decided that the best thing I can do is to stop him.

'I am therefore announcing myself as an independent candidate in the upcoming sheriff election. I intend to fight Guy Gisborne, I intend to beat Guy Gisborne, and I intend to be fairly elected as the next Sheriff of Nottingham.'

'Amazing, amazing, amazing!' Robin blurted, squirming with excitement. 'Did you know about this?''

'Absolutely not,' Zoe said.

The media and the crowd were so shocked by the announcement that the air went quiet, like everyone was taking a big breath. By the time the journalists had thought of questions to ask Ardagh, it was too late. Excited protestors surged up the court steps, knocking the cameras out of the way as they chanted, 'Ardagh Hood, Ardagh Hood!'

Ardagh was short and soon got engulfed by cheerful protestors. The ones in front wanted to shake hands and the ones behind slapped him on the back. Little John worried that his dad would get knocked down the steps, and used his huge frame to open a path through the sea of bodies towards Zoe's car.

'Be safe, be sensible!' Little John pleaded. 'Let my dad through!'

A journalist stuck a big orange microphone in Little John's face. 'John Hood, you're live on News 24. Your father is running for sheriff as an independent, but your girlfriend's father is People's Party candidate for sheriff, and your mother is People's Party candidate for president. Who will you be supporting?'

'I'm neutral,' Little John said, as he used one of his enormous arms to swat away a protestor who was trying to get Ardagh to sign a baseball cap. 'I don't do politics.'

'Ardagh,' another journalist shouted over the crowd. 'Will you condemn criminal activities undertaken by your son, Robin? And how do you think his behaviour reflects upon you as a parent?'

'We will hold a proper press conference tomorrow morning,' Tybalt said, as he pushed through the crowd towards the red car. 'But Robin Hood is a wanted outlaw and my client has been released on a good behaviour bond. Ardagh Hood will not be allowed to have any contact with his younger son.'

As Tybalt said this, Little John opened the back door of the red Porsche coupé and Ardagh settled in the seat, with Robin in the trunk behind. When Tybalt, Ardagh and Little John were all inside the car, Zoe started the motor and began edging through the crowd, which was chanting 'Vote Ardagh' while jubilantly slapping the roof and taking pictures through the tinted rear windows.

Once they were out of the alleyway and into Civic Square, the crowd thinned. Protestors stood back and clapped as the big red Porsche picked up speed.

The only people who didn't seem happy were the Locksley police. They menacingly banged their riot shields against the ground as the car went past. One cop who made a throat-slitting gesture towards Zoe got immediate justice, as a sprinting protestor flung a bag of flour in her face.

There were no crowds once they exited Civic Square and hit the on-ramp for the cross-town highway. The armrest in the centre of the rear seat had an opening that was meant for skis. Ardagh pulled this open and peeked at Robin, lying in the dark.

'Well, fancy finding you back there,' Ardagh said cheerfully.

Tybalt looked back and laughed as Robin tried to squeeze through the rectangular hole.

'Sheriff Hood sounds good to me,' Robin told his dad. 'Can you get me pardoned for all my robberies?'

'Only presidents get to issue pardons,' Little John pointed out. 'If my mum wins the election in April, I'll put in a good word.'

'God help us if that happens.' Robin groaned, then realised that his hips were bigger than the opening. 'I think I'm stuck.'

Little John couldn't resist flicking Robin's ear while he was wedged. Then the giant hooked his fingers through the belt loops on the back of his little brother's trousers and gave an almighty tug.

'OWW, OWW, OWW!' Robin protested. 'You're giving me a wedgie.'

But somehow Robin's bum squished through the opening and he catapulted forward, landing headfirst in the footwell between his dad and his brother, his muddy boots flailing in Little John's face.

Ardagh enjoyed seeing his boys messing around, and tears welled in his eyes. As Robin slid onto the back seat between his dad and his brother, a fond memory made him lean sideways and put his head in his father's lap. Ardagh understood and began laughing.

'You *always* did that when you were a toddler,' Ardagh said tenderly. 'I'm surprised you remember.'

Little John saw that Robin's T-shirt had ridden up to his armpits. He gave the bared belly a gentle slap, then affectionately left his giant hand in place.

'I spent many hours imagining this moment,' Ardagh said, while happy tears streaked his face.

Robin felt like a little kid again as he tipped his head back and watched Locksley's rusty streetlamps skimming by.

He knew things couldn't stay like this. Little John would go back to his boarding school and girlfriend, his dad had an election to win, and Robin would return to the safety of Sherwood Castle. But for a few precious moments, Robin shut out all of the complicated stuff and thought about how much he loved his family.

Look out for

ROBIN HOOD

PRISONS, PARTIES & POWERBOATS

Read on for an extract . . .

COMING NEXT . . .

It's springtime in Sherwood. After a brutal winter, Will Scarlock's rebels are gaining strength, with more members, organised security teams and steady supplies of food and equipment to their base inside the abandoned Sherwood Castle Resort and Casino.

Things look good for Robin too, reunited with his friend Alan Adale and chilling in the castle penthouse with girlfriend **Josie Longshanks**.

Meantime, Ardagh is freshly released from prison and running a popular campaign to beat Guy Gisborne and get elected as the next Sheriff of Nottingham.

But life for our thirteen-year-old hero isn't perfect. Guy Gisborne has upped the bounty on Robin's head to one million pounds, while his friend Marion Maid is locked up in Pelican Island Prison, where she faces daily violence and bullying.

Worst of all, national elections are less than six weeks away. Despite numerous scandals, Nottingham's outgoing sheriff, Marjorie Kovacevic, still has a narrow lead in the race to become president. And she's promised to wipe out Robin and the rebels if she wins.

2. VALUABLE WORK EXPERIENCE

Marion Maid was four hours into a six-hour shift. Her body was slick with sweat and trapped inside a plastic overall that went from her head to her white rubber boots. One of the few good things about being a prisoner was free healthcare, and she wore a foam leg brace following surgery to straighten her crooked right leg.

The brace itched as she walked along a shiny metal gantry. Below were two giant food mixers, like you'd find in any kitchen, except the bowl was bigger than a car and the mixing paddle the size of a door.

Pelican Island Prison's meat processing plant had a central control room and each mixing job arrived with detailed instructions on a touchscreen. First, Marion sterilised the vast mixer by turning a valve and releasing a blast of superheated steam.

While the steam hissed and swirled, she read the ingredient list and gathered items from racks of metal shelves behind: four twenty-kilo bags of salt, thirty kilos of celery powder, twelve litres of autolysed yeast extract, two large tubs of mustard powder and a bucket of sodium erythorbate.

The prison restricted inmates' access to blades, so Marion had a frustrating job opening each hefty bag by lifting it up and catching it on a wall-mounted hook. As the steam from the mixer's sterilisation cycle wafted away, she began emptying sacks and tins over the edge of the gantry into the vast bowl.

Next came the gross bit. While Marion worked on preservatives and seasonings, male inmates working on the upper level had prepared one and a half tonnes of animal products. The mixture varied for each batch, from minced pork for posh sausages to the gruesome fat and mechanically recovered sludge that went into bargain burgers.

When Marion hit the **MIXTURE READY** button on the touchscreen, a giant overhead chute opened and meat, and fat and glossy foaming blood splattered from above. She reached up with a long metal oar to knock down a slab of mince that had stuck in the chute, then turned on the mixing paddle. Slow to begin, then building speed as three huge blocks of fat turned to paste.

'How's my best girl today?' a prisoner named Paul shouted down the chute.

'I'll live,' Marion sighed, as she looked up the metal chute at Paul's blood-smeared boots and overall.

'Are you feeling educated?' Paul asked.

Marion smiled behind her plastic visor. 'My brain gets bigger by the minute,' she said dourly.

This was a joke because young offenders like Marion were supposed to get an education. But Pelican Island was run for profit and King Corporation's management had decided that teenagers could be educated with thirty hours a week of work experience.

'You off shift soon?' Paul asked, as he grabbed a handle to close the chute and start on the next batch.

'Not soon enough,' Marion sighed.

She blinked sweat out of her eyes and occasionally used the oar to push down blobs of meat that stuck to the side of the shiny bowl. When the mix had an even colour and no lumps, she pushed a button to retract the mixing paddle, then switched on a pump.

The mixer sounded like a giant farting vacuum cleaner as the meat paste got sucked down a pipe to an adjoining room, where prisoners turned Marion's mixtures into burgers, sausages, hot dogs and meatballs.

The most physical part of the job came next: going down into the bowl and blasting all the meaty gunk off with a ferociously hot steam wand. But it took a while for all the mix to get sucked out, and while Marion's workstation didn't have a chair, she'd made herself a place to sit by stacking salt bags in a gap between shelves.

Workers were only supposed to drink during hourly breaks, so Marion glanced about furtively before flipping up her visor and downing half a litre of tepid water from a rinsed-out paprika tin.

She shut her eyes, but before getting any rest she heard boots squeaking on the steps up to the gantry. She feared getting told off for slacking by Kerry the floor supervisor, but as Marion stumbled to her feet she realised it was far worse.

3. CHILLI SQUID GAMES

Little John swung through the double doors of a banqueting suite, taking in a space with bay windows overlooking the hotel's rose garden. An elaborate buffet had been set out on a table that ran the room's full length.

'Giant shrimp and caviar,' Clare said keenly.

'Decent spread,' John agreed, as a hotel waiter looked guiltily from his phone and scuttled out through a service door.

John skewered a shrimp as big as his thumb and headed for the chocolate fountain.

'You're such a child!' Clare laughed, as John ran the shrimp under molten chocolate and popped it in his mouth.

'Vile,' John admitted, grinning and coughing as he took a napkin to wipe chocolate off his chin stubble.

As John lifted a plate off a stack, Clare felt her phone vibrate. The screen indicated a video call from her mate Amber, but she got a shock when she answered.

'Wassup, Gisborne!' Robin Hood said cockily. 'Long time no speak-o!'

'How are you showing as Amber?' Clare spluttered as John looked at the screen over her shoulder. 'Did you hack me?'

'Amber's account was in a data breach a few months back,' Robin explained. 'Tell her to change her password.'

'You destroyed my parents' house and *terrified* my little brothers,' Clare growled. 'I'm so not talking to you.'

'Don't hang up!' Robin begged. 'I have to tell Little John something urgent, but he's not answering.'

John patted the pockets of his tracksuit and looked worried. 'I had my phone in the car . . .'

Clare tutted as she passed him her phone.

'Chat soon, Clare-pops,' Robin teased cheerfully. 'Kissy kiss!'

'You're a creepy worm!' Clare shouted.

'Thanks for winding up my girlfriend,' Little John said, scowling at Robin as he took the phone. 'What's so urgent?'

Instead of answering, Robin started howling with laughter. 'What is that tracksuit you're wearing?'

'It's Matt Holland boutique,' John answered. 'Probably cost more than your entire wardrobe.'

'Looks like someone ate a load of carrots then puked down your front.'

'Get to the point,' John sighed. 'Clare's furious, and now you're annoying me.'

'I wasn't expecting you to rock up at your mum's press briefing,' Robin said. 'I need to tell you something in private, away from Clare.'

John glanced around the room looking for cameras. 'Are you stalking us?' he asked.

'Don't speak to him,' Clare urged, then looked angrier as John turned to face one of the bay windows so she couldn't hear.

Robin grunted. 'You think I'd bother stalking you, bruv? First, you're not that important. Second, if I logged in and saw you and Clare doing it, I'd be scarred for life.'

'What's this about?' John asked, speaking quietly, aware that Clare was steaming because he'd not ended the call.

'Don't eat chilli squid from the buffet,' Robin said.

John had an epiphany as he glanced about and spotted a large bowl of chilli squid on the buffet table. 'Are you behind the chaos downstairs?'

'The rebels' finest work,' Robin answered proudly, then launched into an explanation without being asked for one. 'Sheriff Marjorie was hot favourite to become president, but scandals and screw-ups have squeezed her opinion poll lead to almost zero.

'She hired a new public-relations company to stop the rot, but they have *terrible* cybersecurity. My hacking skills are only average, but it took minutes to breach their server and access *every* document, phone and email.'

John nodded, while warily eyeing Clare's scowl and folded arms. 'So that's why the computers can't print name badges, screens are showing episodes of *Property Hunt* and there are seven truckloads of brown balloons?'

'The balloons!' Robin laughed. 'I forgot about them. I'd *love* to be a fly on the wall when Marjorie finds out she's spent a hundred grand on poo emoji balloons!'

John sounded curious. 'How do you know I'm not gonna walk downstairs and tell my mum what you've done?'

'You tell everyone you're not taking sides,' Robin answered. 'If you grass me up to your mum, you'd be crossing that line. Besides, the damage is done – her people must know they've been hacked by now.'

'You're a clever little dickhead,' John admitted. 'And *fine*, I won't tell Mum. But what's this about the squid?'

'I had no idea you'd be at the conference,' Robin said. 'But apparently chilli squid is your ma's favourite.'

'She always orders squid in restaurants,' John agreed.

'We have an insider in the hotel kitchen,' Robin explained. 'Anyone who eats that squid will be spending a week on the toilet, instead of the campaign trail.'

'That's nasty,' John snapped. 'She is my mum, you know.'

Robin turned angry. 'If *your* mum becomes president, she's promised to jail me for life and use the army to blast every rebel and immigrant out of Sherwood Forest. I'd have put something deadlier than salmonella in her squid. But Will Scarlock says rebels won't win by sinking to Marjorie's level and committing murder.'

John groaned with frustration. 'So I'm supposed to stand in a room while my mum and her campaign staff eat poison?'

'I risked everything to warn you when you walked into the buffet,' Robin told his brother. 'I didn't want you getting sick, but go snitch if you like. At least if you do, we'll *finally* know whose side you're on.'

Robert Muchamore's books have sold 15 million copies in over 30 countries, been translated into 24 languages and been number-one bestsellers in eight countries including the UK, France, Germany, Australia and New Zealand.

Find out more at
muchamore.com

Discover more books and sign up to the Robert Muchamore mailing list at muchamore.com

f muchamore

⊙ muchamorerobert

🐦 @robertmuchamore

Thank you for choosing a Hot Key book.

If you want to know more about our authors and what we publish, you can find us online.

You can start at our website

www.hotkeybooks.com

And you can also find us on:

We hope to see you soon!

Robert Muchamore's
ROBIN HOOD series

More ROBIN HOOD adventures to come!